OSHIBANA COMPLEX

Craig Hallam

Published by Inspired Quill: September 2020

First Edition

Contact the author through their website: craighallam.wordpress.com

Chief Editor: Sara-Jayne Slack
Cover Design: Matt Barnes (www.mattseffbarnes.com)

Typeset in Minion Pro

Paperback ISBN: 978-1-908600-97-4
eBook ISBN: 978-1-908600-98-1
Print Edition

Printed in the United Kingdom
1 2 3 4 5 6 7 8 9 10

Inspired Quill Publishing, UK
Business Reg. No. 7592847
www.inspired-quill.com

Praise for Craig Hallam

[Old Haunts is full of] Adventure, comedy, fiendish machines, dire plots and desperate heroism, with a charming side-order of subverting the action tropes. An excellent read.

– Nimue Brown,
author of *Hopeless, Maine*

[In Greaveburn], Hallam has crafted an engaging narrative with likable characters and a climax which makes a statement about human nature. However, one could argue the city itself is the real star of the story. Hallam's expert use of imagery helps us to imagine Greaveburn as a Gothic metropolis full of splendour.

– S. Kinkade,
author of *God School*

Greaveburn is such a rich literary tapestry it would be a shame not to dip our toes into it at least once more. Fans of George R. R. Martin's Game of Thrones *and Mervyn Peake's* Gormenghast *are certain to enjoy getting to know Greaveburn and its residents.*

– Angharad Welsh,
Cotswold Style Magazine

[In Not Before Bed], rest assured, there's something for everyone and each short story is unique as the last. Sheer brilliance this, one of the funniest horror collections I've ever read.

– Nathan Robinson,
author of *Ketchup on Everything*

Hallam puts so much into his writing and certainly produces entertaining and believable characters as well as thrilling plot lines. If you like adventure, fantasy or the Steampunk genre then Alan Shaw is a truly brilliant read.

– Occasionally Adulting

To those who fight for the future, find kinship in dissimilar faces, and love without boundaries.

OSHIBANA COMPLEX

A lone barnacle clings to a rock; its shell is both its home and its world.

Waves crash upon it.

Even in the throes of its death, it will cling, and long after it has gone the shell remains to show others that it was there.

Perhaps it knows that it is finite and strives for something permanent after its inevitable demise; a monument to its existence.

Perhaps it believes its impulses to be something more complex, perhaps it thinks of nothing; only instinct drives it.

Such is humanity; existing solely beneath a tinted shell which stands against the solar winds that have stripped this planet clean.

PART I
Designation

1

THE TUBE'S MILKY white interior blocked out all distractions. No sight, no sound, and Xev's Access, tuned to the Burger Stop company channel, gave nothing but orders and updates in Miyahara's nerve-racking bark. The inner of Xev's uniform had gone from nipple-shattering cold to an unpleasant slickness as eir sweat coated the inside of the polymer material. A hot throb pulsed in eir lower spine, and eir feet cramped at odd intervals, but the tube left no room for slouching, and Miyahara would be watching through Xev's Access, eager to hand out a reprimand. It wasn't worth that kisama's attention. So, bobbing on eir toes to warm up eir pinching calves, Xev waited to be summoned from a narrow, featureless world.

A stilted, artificial voice rang out as a customer stumbled through the Burger Stop door.

"Welcome– to Burger Stop."

Several automations kicked in at once. Xev's Access connected with that of the unseen arrival and the customer's pre-sets popped into Xev's vision. E could see that the customer preferred paler skin, lighter hair, and larger eyes than Xev's own. The Access took care of it, projecting a sham around Xev's real life template which appealed to the customer's aesthetic preferences. The tube faded to transparent to reveal a Xev that the customer wanted to see, spine straight, hands clasped so that eir fingers formed a yin yang on the belly of eir plasti-cloth uniform which now emitted a soft glow. Where an invisible seam ran down the front of eir tube, the thick polyglass slid apart and Xev stepped from the platform. Bowing as e spoke through a company policy smile, even eir voice was re-modulated into something softer, almost apologetic:

"Thank you for choosing Burger Stop. How may I help you today?"

With a brushed steel briefcase white-knuckled to eir side, plastic tie tugged down from an open collar and coffee-stain rings around eir eyes, the customer looked like e might just collapse before e found a table. Wiping one hand down eir face, carelessly smudging eir makeup, the customer muttered something about a table for one. E looked uncomfortable in that expensive suit and Xev could make out the stain of yellowing sweat around eir collar.

Corp type, Xev thought, recognising the haunted look

of an overworked synth who slogged for the Takano-Stanhope corporation.

"Follow me, please."

It had taken weeks of practice to perfect the effortless glide with which Xev drifted across the pearlescent Burger Stop floor; weeks to master the simple and yet robotically perfect back and forth from door to tables. How the little uniform slippers hadn't worn ruts in the tiles by now, e had no idea.

Past chromium plated tables Xev led the customer, whose eyes winced against the floor's dazzling shine. Synths of every kind cluttered the Burger Stop tables: studded bikers and Corp suits, career gamers with hollow cheeks and xp to burn and It-synths with layer upon layer of Access sham filters coating their base template with holographic adornments. At a circular table with red leather seating, Xev held out one hand, briefly, before refastening it to the other.

"Take a seat, if it pleases—"

A clatter erupted somewhere behind. A plastic tray and, by the sound, a host of pre-packed meals splattered across the Burger Stop floor. Silence crashed down. A soft pat of flesh hit the cold tiles as a young synth in Burger Stop uniform fell to eir knees, tears in eir voice.

"I'm sorry. I'm so, so sorry."

Xev didn't lose a beat.

"—you. And summon us when you are ready to order. Can I help you further?"

The customer tossed the case onto one chair and slumped into another without a word. Xev bowed and drifted away. Back on eir platform, e allowed emself a brief side-glance toward the back of the Burger Stop as the tube slid closed. Just enough time to see the offending synth, Toriq, ushered politely away by the belly-bloated Miyahara, whose greasy smile melted just a second too early as e guided the poor synth through a rear door. A knot of ice crept into Xev's spine as the polyglass waxed milky once more, blocking em from view, the light from eir uniform winking out.

That poor worker was done for sure. Burger Stop had a no-drop policy and that meant the poor synth's designation was now void. E had only been named a week or so. If it had been a few days earlier, e would have been for the shredder. Now it just meant another synth on the street. Xev wasn't sure which was worse. E sighed. The worker had a cute template, at least. Nice and symmetrical. There'd be work if e wanted it bad enough. And it wouldn't be long until e did.

"Welcome– to Burger Stop," the auto-voice sang.

Xev's spine snapped straight, the company smile blinking onto eir face as quickly as the Access automations changed eir entire self, and the cylinder faded around em.

"Thank you for choosing Burger Stop. How may I help you today?"

```
End of designated work period
Begin rest period: 8 hours
```

Xev's Access, tapped straight into eir optical nerve, flashed the words across eir vision. With a happy little trill eir xp value, always at the edge of sight, rose by several hundred points.

5,650 XP

Untying eir chin-length hair from the sprout of ponytail at the base of eir neck, Xev ran fingers through the black strands, sighing at eir scalp's sweet release. The fibre-optics near eir roots flashed electric blue. The uniform hanger shunted back into the locker, door clicking shut, and the sounds of industrious cleaning erupted from inside. The next shift was in and working already, someone inhabiting Xev's tube, other synths shuttling back and forth with trays or waiting for the next customer while feigning robotic inertia for the sake of Company Image. Perish that a robot greets someone, or worse, that real synths act anything less than robotic.

Xev tugged on eir jeans and set them for a sad mood; tiny crystal raindrops began to fall down the hexagonal cells, creating a pixelated splash when they met the stylised curlicues of ocean waves which danced just above eir knees. Sliding a fake leather bolero over a red vest, Xev licked eir thumb and bent to reapply a peeling sticker on the scuffed old army boots; a roughly drawn *A* overlapping the circle that surrounded it.

The door thudded as Xev shoulder-barged eir way out the rear of the Burger Stop, its crystal white interior giving way to the perpetual night of Shika-One City. Boots clanged on the metal steps as e propelled eir exhausted husk up to the alley where hulking bins churned their innards, compacting the Burger Stop's trash to a fine powder. In the alley mouth, silhouetted by the throbbing light from the street beyond, crouched Toriq.

Xev thought about walking past. Right on by. Eir boots would carry em right out of the alley and away into the crowd, all the way home where e could log in peace. But the sound of soft weeping rose from Toriq's shuddering shoulders and, as Xev tried eir hardest to sail by, the poor cooch looked right up at em.

Cute template, Xev thought again, as e regarded Toriq's curving jawline and large, dark eyes. Eir bleached hair swept back from a smooth forehead to flow down either shoulder of the clear plastic jacket that covered eir street clothes. At least e'd bought them since eir naming last week, otherwise e'd be out here naked. Xev could see that the usual soft glow of the Access node in Toriq's neck was completely dark.

"Xev, I messed up."

"That you did." Xev felt the sounds roll around eir mouth as e expressed something other than company script for the first time in twelve hours. It felt good.

"Where can I go?"

"Maybe the belly. You'll get along there."

Toriq's eyes seemed to widen further and further until all Xev could see was emself floating in galaxy-sized pupils.

"Don't look at me like that," e said.

"Please." Toriq reached out a hand to brush Xev's leg. Animated water plipped, the waves disturbed by the contact. "I can't do that. Not now. I'm so tired."

Xev screwed up eir face.

"Strewth. I can't take you in, Toriq. You know that. I'll be undezzed right along with you," e sighed. "Go to the belly. Try to get your Access hacked so at least you have some xp."

The weeping synth nodded.

"Then buy yourself a room for tonight. You look like all hell. You need anyth—If it gets real bad, you have my contact," and e turned away from the figure huddled in the shadows as the sobs choked off Toriq's thank you.

Stood in the alley mouth, Xev fought the urge to look back. If e did, e knew, eir stern façade would melt away. No. E couldn't. Tapping the red glowing dome behind eir ear, e felt eir Access drop the Burger Stop channel and connect to Shika-One's full network like spider feet creeping across eir brain. The node turned blue. E blinked as the assault of throbbing neon that gave Hanabi district its name pulsed into life; a perpetual, holographic light show covering every surface of every high-rise cluster from floor to dome.

"*Hi* Xev—"

Xev jumped hard enough to tweak a muscle in eir already aching back. E growled right at the ad-cast: all wide-shouldered sequins and a glowing grin that didn't even twitch when it spoke. A halo of in-game paraphernalia orbited its abdomen.

"—There's no-one quite like Fortini DLC for getting better value for your xp."

"Strewth. *Ignore*." The ad-cast and its grin winked out of existence. Xev shuddered. Reaching into the pocket of eir bolero, e pulled out the only luxury eir xp could afford – a foil-wrapped pack of bubblegum. Muttering to emself, e popped one strip in eir mouth and began to chew. "Creepy sham. Don't let me down, Marsh."

Swiping eir fingers through the air with practiced motions, Xev surfed eir Access, initiating a bootleg playlist to drown out at least some of the ad-casts that swarmed around em. Every song had been illegally downloaded right into Xev's head, off Access, the titles and artists long since forgotten and replaced by strings of numbers and symbols. Working eir tongue, e blew, a hot pink bubble growing and growing, only to pop, and e pulled it back into eir mouth. An old, old song bypassed Xev's ears, the clipped notes and glass-shatter beats of electronic industria moving directly from eir memory to eir limbic system in a shiver of joy.

Xev stepped into the flow of synths, brushing shoulders with a hundred strangers before taking the same number of steps. As e made eir way through Hanabi, neon holo-signage flashed and rolled, morphed and flowed, their effects mixing into each other like a tonic trip. Glowing golden Pisces fish split apart to swoop over and between the crowd, their translucent blue bubbles bursting the words "Best Hanabi tofu-dogs", only to return and reform above the door of a restaurant. Ad-casts in the latest fashions paced inside a boutique's window, snapping between vogueish poses to some unheard beat. Samurai, one blue, one red, clashed sparking swords in a deadly dance that the crowd sauntered right through, their final crash ending with the blue samurai stood over the red, "Garcia Security" flashing above its head. But to Xev, there was only the song, and blowing bubble after bubble after bubble as e walked.

Eir stomach rumbled for the hundredth time in the last few hours, bringing em back to emself.

Between shop front and shop front, where the mass of synths swarmed across the road, small sloped rooves huffed sweet-smelling fog, helping Xev to locate the nearest food shack. E approached the scratched metal counter and eir Access winked a menu into view. Everything worth eating was only a few less xp than e'd earned the entire day. Except, right at the bottom. Food cubes. Tasteless mousse formed into unsatisfying morsels. Technically edible, sustenance by loose association.

Xev let out a sigh.

Rapping the hut's tin counter, Xev held up three and then two fingers to the stall holder wearing a scuffed old cloth hat and strings of beads piled around eir neck. A moment of pan-tossed sizzling and a carton filled with strips of steaming beef and crispy fries sat before Xev.

Taking out eir bubblegum, e stared at the bright pink morsel for a second, sighing at the loss while so much flavour was left, and stuck it to the underside of the counter. E tucked in with enthusiasm, letting the grease and meat and never-been-potato fill eir stomach. Looking up at the cart's sign, Xev's Access brought up PAY in yellow letters. E waved two fingers over the area and the Access behind eir ear pulsed.

Payment accepted

Eir xp total reduced by several hundred points with a sad little sound. Still, it was worth it.

Wiping eir mouth, e tossed the cheap paper napkin to the ground. A spheroid drone rolled around eir boots, corralled the rolling napkin, and disappeared into the trash space beneath the pavement. Xev watched with a smile. So happy in its little task. Back and forth, back and forth. The same motion that drove Xev half mad. Dipping back into eir bolero, e stared at the last few pieces of gum in the packet for a little longer than was sane.

"It's been a long day. You deserve it." And e popped in another piece. Two in one day. "Sheer frivolity."

Pushing off from the food hut's counter, Xev continued on eir way. The ad-casts and holos swam around em. Eir music could do nothing for the visual interruptions. E continued to mutter eir mantra, "Ignore ignore ignore," between bubblegum pops as e headed toward eir home cluster and, hopefully, Marsh's package.

THE FOOT OF the cluster was home to a pawn shop displaying a red bicycle in a dusty window, a rough old thrift store where Xev bought all e ever wore, and a radiant pink nirvana where Lolitas bought their pastel dream dresses and parasols. Hidden right next to these, a rusty metal grid covered the entrance to the cluster which stretched all the way up to where processed clouds scudded against the starless dome.

Xev Accessed the unlock window. With a clang, the cluster's locks disengaged. Whether synths had died in that piss yellow corridor or just voided themselves, it was hard to tell, but a rotten person stench filled the air. Bile green moss clung between once-white tiles, creeping through the grout millimetre by millimetre in an attempt to make the whole corridor a slimy tube.

Eir Access brought up a list of olfactory upgrades which scrolled down the side of eir vision as e walked. Eir Access could pipe music straight to eir ear, bring up menus and information to eir eyes that e could interact with ar-el just like e would in-game. All for free. But the olfactory upgrades cost a pretty amount of xp. More than e would ever afford. With resignation, Xev pushed on through the smell as fast as e could. The elevator was no better. Worse, if anything, as the brushed steel closet concentrated the smell. But holding eir breath just meant keeping the stench inside and so e breathed steadily, mostly through eir mouth, trying to focus on eir bubblegum's scent as the doors slid closed. A wheel of numbers appeared through eir Access. E span it, stabbing it to a halt on 76 and the elevator gave off a whistle of air as it shot into motion. A few fetid breaths later Xev stepped out into another corridor along which e would find eir pod.

At some point, someone had painted a rooster feather (eir Access search had revealed) across the pod's iris. It was faded now, with a glyphic tag in bright blue graffiti splashed across it, but the sight was a welcome one to Xev's weary bones. E selected OPEN and the iris widened, breaking the feather apart a little at first, and then in one clunking expansion, retracting into the pod's aperture. Inside, iris closed, a single strip of light along the pod's centre winked to life. On reflex, Xev waved the rattling atmo to life. Turning eir face up to the breeze, e breathed deep. The patchouli patch slapped over the outlet filled the room with an earthy tang; not sweet, or even pleasant, but it helped Xev to forget the city's oil and ozone scent.

Identical to every one of the hundreds on this floor, and those mirrored on the storeys above and below from street to dome, the pod was small enough that Xev could touch both walls of the tube-shaped space at once. The pod housed one bunk, small enough to render any sharing impossible. Then there was the window. Taking up the entire wall opposite the iris, a circular pane of polyglass stared, lidless, into the void between clusters which hummed and pulsed with storeys-high ad-casts peering into the pods to get at the juicy consumers inside. At least, that was the idea. With centuries of grime crusted to the windows, curtains were unnecessary. Still, the ad-cast's voices came through just fine, calling Xev's name every waking and sleeping second, begging for eir xp.

"—armour that looks as strong as it is, Xev. Just head to our in-game store—"

"—don't let your xp go to waste on second-rate mods—"

"—no need to be alone, Xev. The right nanipet for you is just 15,000 xp away—"

"—omplete customisation for your template. Never fear meeting yourself again."

As Xev shuddered, eir Access pinged.

Message: Marsh: You're welcome.

The first smile of the day spread across Xev's face. That sneaky cooch had come through after all. Kneeling to a low panel by the door, e popped the housing from a vent which, beyond another cover, led back out to the corridor. There, wrapped in ridiculously floral paper ruined by coils of tape, was the package. Vent closed, Xev flopped down onto the bunk, one leg tucked underneath em, and searched for some place where the tape was thinnest as e blew another pink bubble and popped it. Eventually, with a ratty fingernail, e picked an edge free and began to dissect the wrapping.

An old coffee tin, rusted at the rims but still bearing an image of cascading coffee beans turned this way and that in Xev's eager hands. As e upended the can, something inside slid from end to end with a *shhh-ponk*. Eagerly tearing off the can's cap, Xev tipped its contents onto the bed. No brown grounds or beans, but a small plastic dome which lit blue when Xev tapped the top.

Eir Access pinged.

Upload available: Sender: Marsh
Begin?

With the upload initiated, a red ring appeared around Xev's vision. As e shrugged off the bolero and sent eir boots flying off to thud against the pod's iris, the ring turned to amber, to green.

Ping.

Upload complete

Xev crawled along the bunk and wiped at the window with eir sleeve to very little effect and peered out through the dirt. The blinking and swirling nebulas of Hanabi district's neon were still there, but the ad-casts were gone. No more sham grins and shiny skins. No more xp grabbing holo-sales. Flopping back onto the bunk, Xev let a grin expand into the silence of eir pod, and made a yummy noise at the back of eir throat.

It was time to log.

Making emself comfortable on the bunk, Xev swiped eir hand from right to left, the Access picking up the familiar movement, and one reality traded places with another.

XEV FLOATED. THERE was no ground, no sky – only an unending vista of pure white and the sensation of stretching out, beyond the limits of eir ar-el template's solid form. Savouring the feeling, Xev drew emself further into the game, every twitch of thought diverted from eir ar-el muscles to steer em through the menu space's expanse. Concentrating on where e wanted to be, Xev lurched as gravity reasserted and e was suddenly upright and still. Opening eir eyes, the Access displayed eir in-game stats and levelling progress, a green hp haloing the entirety of eir vision. Only eir xp counter remained between worlds.

Horizons. The game had horizons. At least, this module did. Across a vista of grasslands which rose into warm hills, Xev could see all the way to fog-choked mountain slopes. E scanned around to where the pale sun made a twinkling line of the ocean in the distance. Ar-el, Xev could never see much further than the next cluster, but here, the feel of eir eyes focussing on something so distant felt like stretching after a long time confined.

After continuing to scan for a moment, eir focus came to rest on a spire of ice that scratched the sky, impossibly visible despite the vast distance; the in-game representation of the Takano-Stanhope corporation. The only piece of undeletable code in the base module on which all synths built their vast, virtual wonderlands; an anchor to remind gamers who made all worlds possible. Xev had played modules where it was a star that shone night and day, or a great tree whose lower branches could never be reached. In the Alkia module, it was a spire of ice at the edge of the world.

Xev took in eir form, enjoying the sensation of stepping outside eir own template for the first time that day. E was seven feet tall now, made of dark metal, eir face a high-crowned helm with glowing red eyes. E flexed the segmented gauntlets that were eir hands. When e stretched out eir arms, e felt the squeak and grind of eir joints. Still, e could feel the cool breeze that came in across the rustling grass to lick eir metallic skin. Magic. Drawing a greatsword from eir back, e gave a few practice swings, the blade making deep *whoomph* sounds as it moved effortlessly despite the imposing weight.

A rustle in the grass beside Xev, and there stood Marsh as if e'd never been anywhere else. Eir thin leather armour fluttered for a second as if whipped by the wind, along with the platinum braid which ran down to behind eir knees. Slightly serrated ears twitched and Marsh turned with an impish smile.

"Greetings, Truckface."

"Hello, Shrimpy," Xev rumbled.

Marsh burst into laughter which sounded like birdsong and mountain streams when modulated through eir avi.

"Got your package. Legendary."

"You wanted the best, and you paid some pretty xp for it. You could have upgraded your armour for the shiny mithril skin but you want to waste it on ar-el stuff, who am I to argue?"

"No more ad-casts. That's better than shiny armour. Plus, shiny doesn't mean good. I've seen some real shiny squishies go down way faster than my rusted old hide."

"The Corp ad-casts will upgrade eventually. They'll be back."

"But for now, there's peace. We busting this level tonight or what?"

"Wide open."

Xev Accessed eir menus for a second, a large blue gem appearing in eir hand. As eir gauntlet hand crushed it, their forms shimmered and winked out, leaving only glistening sand to fall to the grass.

2

P*ING*
 Rolling over in eir bunk, Xev's eyes creaked open. Eir Access sent out another ping, followed by a message in glowing yellow text.

```
Good morning, Xev. Your designation begins
at 05:00
That is 1 hour from now
```

With a groan, e sat up, brushing the hair back from eir eyes in a cascade of electric blue. Of course, it was ridiculous, but e swore eir muscles ached from last night's quest. E thought of goblin teeth and was glad e'd chosen a Forged avi. The magical armour body had really come in handy. Both e and Marsh were still a little under the level cap but there was always tonight, and they'd earned enough xp to eat something other than food cubes with a little left over for luxuries. Toilet paper, and a drink that tasted of something, perhaps.

Shuffling from the edge of eir bunk, Xev stretched. E kicked a pad near the floor and a rudimentary bathroom slid out of the pod wall. Tending to eir bladder first, e leant over the sink and swiped on the flow of water. There was just enough to wash the essentials before the flow dried up. Eir Access threw up a window.

```
Would you like more water?
(300 XP)
```

Xev checked eir xp readout, thought for a second, and swiped. That sad, judging trill rang in eir ear.

The flow returned long enough for actual warm water to come through. Stripping completely, e took advantage of every point spent to feel as clean as possible. With the water now cycling through the blistering phase of its flow, it was almost useless again without contracting serious burns. Xev let it flow anyway, breathing in the clean steam and regarding emself in the fogged mirror.

Not for the first time, e wondered who the basis of eir template had been. Who had been the originator of that upturned nose and rounded chin? What about the ears that Xev had decorated with a series of chrome studs? The thick hair, which Xev wore feathered into eir neck, the electric blue fibres showing through as the only augment extravagance e could afford. Xev ran a finger along tattooed symbols connected by a single black line. Whose collarbone was this? That same collarbone e had decorated to distinguish emself from others of the same template.

Not that anyone would want to be em. On the lowest rung of the lowest profession. Living in the back and forth moments from pod to Burger Stop, tube to table. No. No-one would think to steal such a thin existence. Every synth in the city was too busy struggling to be emselves, never mind anyone else.

Not for the first time, Xev wondered where the others of eir template were right now. What were their designations? E'd probably never know. After all, same-template synths tended to avoid each other. Too creep to come across someone wearing your own face in the street. There was only so much that body mods and Access filters could do, after all.

In the drawer, Xev found a scuffed old t-shirt bearing the white curlicues on red background of some long-forgotten logo, which e'd bought from the trusty thrift store. Retro, verging on obscurity, just as e liked it. Then e shucked into the holo-jeans, left to the same drizzle setting as last night. Throwing on eir bolero over it all, e headed out.

Xev found eir eyes drawn upward, as they often were; a habit that e wasn't certain when e'd developed. Perhaps it wasn't eir habit at all. A morning in Shika-One was exactly like an afternoon, an evening, a night. The dome kept out deadly solar rays, but that meant no light, no rain, no stars or moon. There was no telling if that stuff even happened anymore beyond the shell. The only way to experience it was through modules designed by synths who had never seen it either. For all e knew, the universe was dead and the dome floated through a starless void forever and ever with Shika-One in its belly. What Xev knew well was this section of the dome's insides, where there was only the night and Hanabi's eternal neon burlesque. Maybe somewhere else in the city the lights were different, but travel was just one more thing that Xev would never afford.

Ping

```
Message: Marsh: Breakfast?
Reply: You buying?
Message: Marsh: Fat chance.
```

Xev wove eir way through the crowds, reversing last night's course. Without the ad-casts, e could see the other synths more clearly. Eyes became focussed or distant as they Accessed, their fingers making magician motions in the air; surfing, paying, playing catch with their yipping, multi-coloured nanipets. Shika-One's synths strived for variety in every outfit. Dresses of lace and puffed crinoline over stacked and chained boots, studded midriffs, asymmetrical flashes of glittered flesh, lizard-scale vests, halo collars and ink-decorated skin. Xev ducked as a cloud of parasols swept by at eye height, Lolitas dangling beneath. A sham tail protruded from the rear of a silk suit, swishing against eir legs as its owner stalked by. All the richer synths had shams over their faces, clothes, hair, the likes of which Xev only experienced while on Burger Stop Company time. Even without the ad-casts, there was too much of it. Too much of everything.

BESIDE THE OLD food cart, hunched over to sip pale yellow water from a plastic cup, sat a synth with a tall template, hair coifed in a spitfire red wave, eir jacket hand-stitched with embroidered patches of all shapes and colours.

Xev squeezed Marsh's shoulder in greeting.

"Heya. Want some piss water?" Marsh asked. Eir lips. Xev was insanely jealous of those lips. Eir own template had crap lips.

"Think I'll pass."

"Just because it tastes like boot scrape doesn't mean you can go without. You'll drop down dead one of these days."

"Feel free to tempt fate on my account."

"Grump. That why your jeans are raining? Looks like your specials are weeping. Not a good look."

Ignoring eir friend, Xev showed the back of eir hand to the cart owner, ring finger held down with eir thumb. Marsh's might-be-eggs arrived first, but Xev's weren't far behind. With some soy ketchup, they weren't even so bad.

"So, when are you going to let me take you on a harder quest? It's about time we took on a drake or some almighty level stuff like that."

Xev held up a hand.

"I just want to play enough to eat good. What if we get tanked?"

"We'll earn it right back. Wouldn't you like to finally

get that slick jumpsuit you keep trying on in the thrift store?"

"Shut up."

"Shiny shiny," Marsh teased, poking a finger into Xev's ribs who shrugged it away.

"It can twinkle all it likes. I'm not tanking myself broke for nothing."

Marsh pouted with those coveted lips.

"You're even more of a grump than usual."

Shoving an empty plate away, Xev crossed eir arms on the cart counter, and turned eir head to regard the street for a moment.

"Saw some poor cooch lose eir dez yesterday. Wasn't pretty."

Marsh nodded along. "Heard. Naught to be done."

"Still…"

"I know. But you still have yours. Mouths to feed. Xp to earn…"

"I don't even feed no one. Just shuttle them back and forth a ways."

"But you're better than some faceless bot. Least that's what Company brains think and I'm happy for them to keep thinking it. Keeps us in xp, keeps us in Access."

"Keeps us caged up."

Marsh let out a cockerel crow that no single face turned toward. "Come on, my pretty hen. Let's away."

Swiping to pay, their Access gave the lilting tone and they were off.

AT THE MOUTH of the alley to Burger Stop's rear, Xev and Marsh hugged.

"Don't lose your mind in the maze, little one," Marsh said.

"Marsh, I don't think I know the path to start with."

Marsh squeezed a little tighter.

"Secret. Don't tell. None of us do. But we have each other, yes?"

Xev nodded against Marsh's chest. "You're right."

Marsh pulled away with a smile. "I know. But I surely do love to hear it."

As they made to part ways, Xev giving a wink of thinly veiled sadness, a Corp truck rolled right alongside. The truck, twice their height and built as if it could withstand a cluster dropping on it, shuddered to a stop, seeming to ingest Hanabi's lights into the dark void of its armoured hide.

It would make a fine mount for my avi, Xev thought.

From the rear, two Wardens thudded down onto the pavement from the high cab. One circled the truck, pausing only to shove Xev and Marsh aside with eir stave.

"Make room," e barked through the electronics in its faceless helmet.

Wordlessly, they backed a few feet down the alley as the other Warden rolled up the truck's shuttered side to reveal a row of new synths like pale fruit in thin paper overalls. Some of them stepped back into the shadows of the truck's interior, some shaded their eyes from Hanabi's startling neon, others shivered and danced in their bare feet.

"Lookit them synths, shiny and new," Marsh muttered.

"Five years hence that was you stepping off all milky white."

"I was never like that."

"We all were," Xev muttered. "It's only since we got cut loose that we got all dirty."

"I ain't dirty. Speak for yourself." Marsh gave em a look of mock-disgust.

"You the dirtiest cooch I know. That's why you're my buddy."

They squeezed each other's hands and Xev gave a wink but, as the Warden gestured to one of the new synths, memories washed back and e squeezed a little harder.

A synth crept toward the platform edge, stubble-haired and wide eyed. Grabbed by the elbow and forced out of the truck, e almost fell but caught emself at the last moment. Xev felt Marsh wince.

Shutters slammed shut and Wardens back inside, the truck rolled away, bearing the rest of the synths to their destinations across the district. The synth looked around emself. Xev could see its Access, glowing red. The damned Wardens hadn't even linked em to whoever was supposed to collect. Xev and Marsh exchanged glances.

"We're not getting involved," Marsh said.

"Just set em on eir way, that's all," Xev agreed.

Marsh nodded to end the well-practised theatre.

Checking that the truck was very gone, Marsh stepped toward the shiny new synth, who shrank back from Marsh's height and colours, paper overalls rustling, letting out a little yelp of surprise when a cleaning drone rolled past eir foot to collect some discarded noodles.

"S'okay. S'okay," Marsh cooed. But the synth clearly disagreed.

"Aside, you galoot. You're scaring em," Xev said, circling eir larger friend. Turning eir head, e showed the synth eir Access. "See? We're just like you. You need to put your fingers just here." Xev demonstrated, eir Access winking red back to blue.

"They don't even bother showing them how to Access no more," Marsh grumbled.

The new synth reached up gingerly, feeling the small raised area under the flesh of eir neck. The contact was enough to activate and the synth staggered back a little, eyes blinking furiously as the Access hijacked eir optic nerve.

Xev's Access showed the synth's designation.
"Strewth."

Burger Stop - Usher

Marsh laughed, incredulous.
"Looks like you got yourself a new partner."

WITH EIR BACKSIDE holding open the door to the Burger Stop's stainless steel interior, Xev beckoned for the synth to follow em down the dark stairs to the basement entrance.

"C'mon. We have to be inside or we'll get docked. Pods and Access, you get free. But if you want to eat, and find nice warmth things for your feet, you have to work your dez."

The synth rocked on air naked heels, peering into the room beyond the door but not taking a step.

"Serious as the grave. You have to come in or those jackboots will be back to take you away again."

That seemed to do the trick. The synth crept forward, still peering, a rodent whose whole existence had taught it to be suspicious. It was hard to watch. This pastel soft, brand new creature's only knowledge was how scary life was. But, as Xev held out eir hand, the synth learned a different lesson, and their fingers slid together as e was led forward.

Inside the locker room's stainless silver interior, Xev used eir Access to find the synth's allocated locker, a little further down from eir own.

New Synthetic Allocation

"Looks like this is yours. Now, we don't have much time before shift so just watch me, ok?"

The synth seemed to understand what Xev was saying but didn't reply.

Xev sighed. "You'll have to talk eventually, you know. For now, just nod."

The synth obeyed.

"That's a start, I guess." Xev Accessed eir locker door, the synth watching carefully as Xev replaced eir street clothes with a shiver of cold plastic uniform. Before slipping on eir cap, e pinned back eir hair and made sure none would show by the locker's internal mirror.

"Guess you don't have to worry about that part, yet," Xev said. The synth cocked eir bald head.

With one last head-to-toe check in the mirror, Xev turned back to the synth in eir paper overalls. With a hand on each shoulder, Xev sat the synth down on the locker room's chrome bench.

"Just wait here and Miyahara will come see to you." As if summoned by eir name, the Burger Stop owner stormed through the door, already glowering in shiny yellow shirt and pinstripe trousers, eir hair an ink black hedgehog.

When the Burger Stop owner spoke, it was in clipped tones, like the clack of a keyboard. "Xev! That new synth is yours. Sync it up."

Xev's eyebrows crashed together as e began to argue: "But I had the last one—"

"And you'll take another. Now do as you're told or you'll be getting docked. Train it up."

And Miyahara was gone again.

"Damned cooch saves eir xp for a promotion, thinks e owns the damn city," Xev mumbled, making sure e wouldn't be heard.

The synth was looking at em, a little sad.

"Already more involved than I want to be. Nothing personal. Hell, there's nothing about you not to like, or the reverse, just yet. Guess we'll be putting in some hours."

Xev took the synth's unresisting hand and placed its fingertips onto eir own Access before reciprocating the gesture. Both domes of light pulsed.

`Sync initiated`

The synth blinked a few times as a window appeared in its vision which showed itself as Xev saw it.

"Now this'll be a little weird-eird," Xev began. "The echo's just coz we're stood so close-ose. But once I'm up there and you're down here, it'll clean up. Now watch-atch what I do-o, and remember."

Straightening eir uniform one last time, shaking eir head with a smile as the synth copied the motion on its overalls, Xev clasped eir hands ying-yang and stepped into the tube. It hissed closed and the platform rose through the ceiling to eir designation just inside the Burger Stop's door.

3

F OR HALF AN hour out of the next twelve, Xev was released into the locker room to eat. The new synth sat on the cold chrome bench, blinking at the display behind its eyes. Xev didn't say a thing, but took the opportunity to shove a Burger Stop meal into eir mouth and take the weight off eir quivering knees as eir Access counted down every millisecond of break time in glowing red. With a few seconds left, the tube hissed closed and carried em back up to work. The synth watched it all with blank fascination and waited six more hours for Xev to return.

STRUGGLING TO HOLD emself upright, Xev shuffled to eir locker, changed clothes, and beckoned silently to eir new companion as e ducked out the door. As e did, eir xp readout trilled, the number rising by a few hundred points.

"Yay-ay," e stated coldly, taking the stairs up to the alley. With the echo of eir own voice rattling around eir head, Xev cancelled the sync. "Did you get some xp?"

The synth blinked, its eyes darting down to the bottom left as if it might catch the little floating numbers if it was fast enough. It nodded. With a swipe of its fingers, the xp value appeared in Xev's Access. It had evidently been practicing.

200 XP

"Enough for food or clothes but not both. Sounds about right. C'mon. We've got a lot more to do before sleep."

As the synth chomped down thinly sliced pseudo-chicken and gravied vegetables, Xev poked at eir own meal and tried not to fall asleep. Swiping a payment, the day's xp disappeared in one swoop. There'd be no gaming for em tonight either, so no extra xp to spend. At least e had a little saved up.

"Done? C'mon then. We have to go see a friend."

In Xev's wake, the synth's head swivelled like a weathervane, caught on every fascinating breeze of Hanabi's wonders. Xev stalked the scarred concrete sidewalk, barely looking unless someone stepped in eir path. Leading them down an alley between two clusters, the fanfare of Hanabi gave way to crumpled steel bins and vent-tossed trash. Xev's Access changed viewing mode so that the edge of each wall and object appeared as yellow grids, helping em to navigate through the darkness. It also made glowing murder scene outlines where homeless gamers huddled, the eyes in their sunken faces blank with the game.

Xev stepped over a slumped figure.

"Tip one. Stay working. Don't get addicted to the game. Only a talented few can really make it by with game xp alone. The Corp set it up that way. The levels you need to reach to stay fed and warm once you lose your dez and your pod are ones the likes of you and I will never see. Strewth. I forgot about Marsh."

```
Message: Send to: Marsh: Looks like I'm
stuck with this synth. No game for me
tonight. I'm taking it to Tecks. See you
tomorrow.
```

Seconds later:

```
Message: Marsh: Good luck. Don't let the
belly getcha.
Reply: Would you come save me?
Message: Marsh: Fat chance. There's no xp
gain in ar-el quests. You're getting rescued
by no-one.
```

Turning a series of corners, what remained of Hanabi's background hubbub fell away until they could have been anywhere in Shika-One's seasonless expanse. Their feet tore through dunes of trash, left where the cleaning drones would never go for fear of being swiped for their internal components. Xev looked back at eir companion, whose eyes were darting between every alcove and corner and shadow. With a sigh, Xev brought up a map of the city and shared it. Apart from a tiny section near the upper right corner, the whole thing was a pixelated blur.

"See that? Your Access won't let you see anywhere you can't travel to. Short version, you're stuck where they put you, unless you can buy your way there. Lucky we're going to a place off-map. Although you won't hear folks say out loud, everyone comes here." Xev carried on through the litter drifts. "And don't worry about Wardens. They're synths, just like us. And every synth needs the belly at some point so they leave it be. Still, don't repeat what you see down here, ok? You see someone in the belly, don't mean you know them outside. That's tip two. We're here."

A gelatinous blue light bathed them as they stepped from one alleyway to another of a very different kind. Forgotten rear doors of the colossal clusters had been recycled into shuttered shop fronts promoting their wares with paint signs on lean-tos of sheet metal. Occasionally, a single slash of ar-el neon underlined a whitewash word. A faint umber leaked out of doorways and windows, lighting the belly's backstreets with an uneasy glow. Music pumped out of a doorway as they passed, the sign offering to fulfil Same-Template Fantasies and Access-Enhanced Experiences.

Many of the belly synths had lost their designation, their pod, and their right to Access, and as a result had migrated to where people relied on the game to stay fed.

Only, the game was never meant to fund an entire ar-el existence, only supplement it. Many synths in these parts were round-the-clock gamers, using tonics to keep their minds awake while their bodies rested so that they might continue to crunch for precious xp. Access could be hacked, of course, but only so far as Takano-Stanhope would look the other way.

The belly synths had a cobbled together, erratic style all of their own as Access shams and filters weren't an option for the undezzed. These alienated synths moved in the gloom, chatted in corners, laughing and puffing blue smoke from their ringed and spiked nostrils. Makeup in humming neon gradients slashed across faces, or exploded around heavily darkened eyes, cutting into cheekbones and lips with rainbow hues. Dermal implants created braille patterns on faces and hands, nails and irises dyed all colours, their clothes and wild hair were punches of colour in the dark. Xev spotted one or two synths whose collar tattoos were overlaid with a neat rectangle of shiny scar tissue; those who believed that the belly was just another part of the Takano-Stanhope system and that their naming day tattoos weren't a rebellious act of individualisation at all but just another barcode on their body to be categorised by. Xev found eir own tattoo itching at the thought of having it burnt off.

"How fresh is that synth?" a voice cut out of the dark at them.

The new synth flinched behind Xev, who cast an

uncertain glare into the shadows where a green glow hovered around shoulder height.

"Not for sale. Off with you," Xev snapped.

The voice's owner stepped forward, light sliding across a black PVC jumpsuit, eir face under-lit by the glowing green tube which exited one tattooed collarbone only to dive into the neck inches away.

"Nasty nasty. No need for that," e rasped. "I'd pay more xp than you make in a year for a fresh synth like that one."

As the buyer circled around them, Xev put emself between em and the synth.

"Khsss." A hiss burst from Xev that made the synth wince.

The buyer clicked eir tongue and swirled away, one green-veined eye twitching as e disappeared.

"Tonic sharks," Xev said, partly to emself, partly to the synth. "Guess what tip three is."

Through catcalls and leaden gazes, they approached a building a little more orderly than the others. The façade, oddly devoid of graffiti, its shutter hung properly, and only a single word hand-painted above the red doorway:

Library

Xev ducked inside with the synth, finding themselves in something akin to a foyer with a spread of red carpet not cut for the room's edges. Past mismatched wooden chairs and motheaten wall hangings, through a toothless doorway to a dark corridor beyond, they found concrete steps spiralling downward.

"This is where you'll learn to be a real person. By the time you hit your naming day, you'll be all up to speed."

They descended into a low-ceilinged cellar where booths had been built from all manner of leftovers, leaving an aisle down the centre choked with thick cables that led away into the dark. "Tecks can get you pretty much anything from the Takano-Stanhope archives. Movies, music, books and old entertainment shows. All for free. Even the stuff that they keep locked up tight. It'll help you learn about something other than the nothing at Burger Stop."

In each booth sat a synth, a cable attached to their Access, eyes distant with whatever they were viewing. Some laughed along with old movies, others bopped to long forgotten songs as they committed them to personal storage.

"I'll be right back. Wait here."

Further along the row, where the cables ran, Xev found Tecks seated behind a bank of conduits in a hardware haven. From behind, eir wild hair made a crest above the chair back, silhouetted by the screens' glow. Eir hands moved sensually through the air as e Accessed each synth's feed, shunting and queueing content.

"Tecks, You in?"

"I am indeed 'in'," the Librarian answered, eir voice a calming lilt.

"Brought a new synth for booth seventeen."

"You want me to come hook it up?"

"I can do it."

"I'll shoot it the basics. You come back down here when you're done. I got real hot chocolate."

"Sounds clean."

Heading back to the booth, Xev found the synth still staring at the spot e'd been a few minutes before.

"Get comfy. You're going to be here a while."

Leaning over, e took the Access diverter from its hook on the wall. Peeling the cover from an adhesive jelly pad, Xev applied it to the synth's Access, followed by the diverter. "The Corp don't let us watch anything they don't want us to, so we have to bypass the security in your Access. Enjoy it. Wish I could watch it for the first time again. Be back when it's done."

As e left, the synth watched em go, eyes losing focus as the Access kicked in.

Tecks didn't turn to look as Xev took a stool in the corner, eir hands still conducting invisible orchestras. Through eir own Access, Xev could see the feeds like swarming birds around Tecks' head but couldn't keep up with the flow of information. Only the librarian could do that.

"Chocolate's in the flask," Tecks said.

Xev shuffled on the hard little stool, back propped against the wall. But the cup of hot brown sweetness was sublime.

"You want me to load you something?" Tecks' voice drifted over.

"Sometimes the quiet is nice."

"Quiet's for thinking. You don't want to think too hard. You might just come up with something. Last person had an idea got shredded," Tecks said with the soft neutrality of a rising cloud.

Xev smiled to emself as e let the peace roll over em, the soul-warming scent of chocolate filling eir head.

"I'll be careful."

XEV JERKED AWAKE to the sound of Tecks' voice.

"Easy there. Your new buddy needs some rest, methinks. The download's slowed right down. Looks like you could use a little, too."

"When you going to figure out how to download this stuff while we sleep?"

"Soon as the laws of physics change, I'll get right on it."

Xev grunted. "How much does e have?"

"I put in the history basics, and the social stuff. Balanced it with a little music. I managed to cram in a lot. That synth's got a good sponge."

Although tired, Xev placed a mock-shock hand on eir mouth. "Better than mine?"

Tecks gave em a smile with teeth only on one side.

"Ain't no one perfect."

Tecks turned back to eir feeds and Xev rose to leave.

The synth sat rod straight and wide-eyed, face a little pale. Eir eyes refocussed as Xev disconnected the diverter.

"That was something to see, huh?"

The synth tilted its chin up to Xev, eyes shimmering with tears, brow bunched and breaths shuddering from its chest.

"Oh." Crouching to the synth, Xev laid a hand on the synth's where it perched on shivering knees. "It's much, I know. Bad things happen. I wish I could say it's ok now, but now you know the hows and whys of Shika-One."

The synth gave a stunted, chilly nod.

"We just keep on. All of us. Okay? What about the music? The music's good, right?"

A weak smile broke through the shock.

"Good. Well, Tecks has lots of that. And other stuff, too. We'll download all you want, bit by bit. We've had a long day and tomorrow will be just the same. Let's get some sleep."

THE SYSTEM REALLY *had* made sure that Xev was stuck with the synth. With a quick glance at eir pod designation, Xev sighed and led the way; all the way to eir own cluster, five floors above eir own pod.

The iris slid-clunked open, the light flickering on.

"Here we go." Xev gave the synth a little pat on the back which turned to a light shove when it refused to step inside. "Your Access will show you around. Get some sleep. I'll meet you downstairs in a few hours to head back to work. Try to sleep. If you fall asleep at the Burger Stop they—"

They'll shred you good.

"—you'll be in big trouble."

The synth turned back to the door, making to follow as Xev left, but e swiped for the iris to close, shrinking to block the watery look that the synth gave em as e stepped away. E massaged eir tired brow, letting out a sigh that could shake foundations.

Tomorrow. We'll start again tomorrow.

4

"OKAY-AY. WHILE I'M gone, review the company policy files. You'll need to know every word and be able to spit it up-tup."

The synth nodded despite its eyes being trained on its knees.

"I better get up there-ere."

The synth carried on regarding its knees, or maybe it was the ratty old pair of tiny black slippers that Xev had donated to it which were only just better than bare feet. With the hiss and swish of the tube platform's exit, the synth wiped its damp cheek and Accessed the company file pulsing in the centre of its vision. With prepacked words scrolling and scrolling before its eyes, it began to hum an old tune; one that it shouldn't know.

THE PLATFORM ROSE, carrying Xev into the tube. For all e

knew, the Burger Stop was heaving with people. For all e knew there was no one there at all. There was only the curved white world of the tube.

"Welcome– to Burger Stop."

A whip-crack of spine and smile, flicker of sham, hush of tube.

"Thank you for choosing Burger Stop. How may I help you today?"

The high collar and broad shoulders of the synth's dress, coupled with a lopsided wave of hair and ar-el makeup drawing attention to an exquisite jawline told Xev that this was an It-synth, the kind who rode the ever-thinning line between designation and hedonistic escape. Dark spots under the eyes told the rest of the tale, the tonics showing in the faintest of green glow at the tear ducts. Last night's makeup wasn't doing much to hide it at all.

"I'm starving. Table for one."

The company channel flashed a map of the Burger Stop through Xev's Access. It was almost as full as full could be, with only one seat free.

"Follow me, please."

As usual, every texture and colour filled the Burger Stop's tables. Explosions of hair and clothing; long, dark things with heavy-lidded eyes; dishevelled party-hards on their way home; neat Corp types on their way out. Xev drifted through them all, feeling the new synth's sync at the back of eir mind as an unscratchable itch. At the long windows that made up one wall, e gestured to a high bench with tall stools.

"Take a seat, if it pleases you. And summon us when you are ready to order. Can I help you further?"

The It-synth didn't answer, hopping onto the stool, squirming to tug down the dress with one hand and swiping the call option with the other. As Xev gave a bow and moved away, one of the server synths was already moving in behind em.

E was just about to step into the tube when eir Access forced its way into the foreground of eir awareness.

Every synth in the Burger Stop sat a little more upright. Teeth froze mid-bite, drinks paused halfway up the straw. Every pair of eyes widened, unfocussed.

The news feed kicked in.

A burst of light. More light than Xev had ever seen. Not from a sign or a lamp, but an all-encompassing light that sizzled the skin as soon as it touched.

High over rolling crop fields, a diffuse orb of brilliant white shone beyond a deep brown dome. Huge machines groaned back and forth below, picking, spraying. As the viewpoint rotated, scanned, searched, the immense hulk of the Shika-One dome passed in the near distance and was gone.

I'm outside. In the secondary dome.

The view dived. Fast. Xev's stomach lurched as the camera drone swooped over acres and acres of soybean stalks. There, below, a trail cut through the lush green rows. And more, more trails behind it, converging.

The perspective shifted again. The fields rushed all around. Xev could feel breath hot in eir chest, could feel the strain of eir heart. Plants whipped at eir knees as e fought to stay upright, stumbling through the ploughed ruts, splattering soil on the white paper of eir overalls.

Ahead, shacks reflected the... the *sunlight* from their bleached walls, and synths in wide hats, their skins coated in some kind of thick and cracking white paint, stood aghast, looking right at em.

The brittle earth, dry and unyielding, thudded under eir feet as e ran. The synths parted as e approached, some shoving others behind them, uncertain, their dark eyes peering out from white masks of fear.

Schracckk.

Xev spasmed as hot pain exploded across eir shoulder blades. Red droplets filled the air as the news feed slowed, slowed, spooling out the moment in an agonising thread. Deep red explosions splashed across the hungry ground. The onlooking synths reeled, screaming in slow-motion. And Xev was turning, falling, hitting the ground as more detonations exploded across em.

Perspective shift.

Now from above, jerking back by a few seconds for the replay. A synth darted through the field, paper overalls hanging in ribbons, bald head and naked face crackling, reddening by the second as the sun, only partially filtered through the secondary dome's brown shield, touched it for the first time. The Wardens came next. Three of them, black-clad attack dogs, rifles raised. The first shot exploded through the synth, spinning em. The second and third took eir fall and turned it into a meteor strike, slamming em into the ground. Screams from the assembled workers filled the air. The drone swooped low as the synth leaked onto the ground, steam rising from the corpse as the sun boiled its fluids as they emerged.

Snap back.

Xev could feel emself falling. Eir ribs hit the chrome side of a Burger Stop booth, and e grabbed for it, managing to keep eir feet. All around, synths gasped for air, fell from their stools, fought to run from something and then realised where they were. Food and drink dribbled from stunned mouths or was spat out to the taste of someone else's blood. Beyond the window, bedlam. Synths reeled and clung to each other in the street. Tears fell and senseless words battered the air. Xev scrambled, stumbled, made eir way to the tube which closed and waxed opaque around em.

In the curved white world, e panted, eir mouth filled with the taste of copper. Xev swiped the Access to descend. *Descend.*

But it wasn't time to rest. Not yet. And the tube wouldn't go.

Crumpling as far as e could, Xev's knees and back squeaked on the tube's too-narrow sides. Half up and half down, e sobbed, knowing that no one outside could see.

HISSING, THE TUBE descended, bearing Xev down to the locker room. As it slid open, e stumbled out, knees like jelly. Holding on to the lockers for support, even eir fingers seemed loose in their joints.

The new synth was gone.

Snapping eir head around, Xev's pulse raced for the second time that day.

"Where'd you go?"

E darted around the small room, checking under the bench, in the corner by the exit. But the synth was nowhere to be seen. The outer door wouldn't open without it being time. Miyahara's office would open for only em. There was nowhere for em to—

The sync.

Xev flipped the link, so e could see what the synth saw.

Darkness. *Total* darkness, to the degree that Xev wondered if the connection had been made at all.

And then e turned, slowly, eyes narrowing on the lockers.

New synthetic allocation

"Strewth."

Crouching, Xev knocked on the locker door, real gentle.

"Hey. Hey in there."

No answer, but a shuffle of movement linked up with a slight shift in the sync window. Xev flopped down cross-legged before the locker. E'd sat many times with Marsh like this. Companions driven to exhausted consolation. When e spoke again, e lowered eir voice to a caring lull. Eir own blurred reflection mimicking em in the locker door.

"I can't make you come out, but if Miyahara has to come unlock this thing—"

Clunk.

The locker opened a crack. Water spilled out, soaking Xev's bottom where e sat. Then there was the new synth, knees up under its chin. Soaking wet and covered in suds.

Xev clapped a hand over eir mouth to stifle the laughter.

"Oh. Get caught in the wash cycle?" And that was it. With the words made manifest, Xev exploded. Gasping laughter and rivulets of tears. Sat on the locker room floor, holding eir face as if it might burst, rocking and chuckling as the new synth's blank, distraught face looked out from beneath a crown of foam.

Through the fading tinkle of giggles, Xev managed to speak.

"The feed spooked you, huh?"

The synth nodded.

Xev tried to pull emself together. E shuffled closer, kneeling in front of the synth in cold water and suds.

"Hey, well, you know that was a long way from here. Not even under the same dome. The forced sync just makes it feel like it's right here." E tapped eir forehead. "Don't worry. They don't happen often. Takano-Stanhope just like to make a point now and then, is all. Me and you, who stay where we are, we're safe as safe can be."

E held out eir hand, and the synth took it.

5

X EV KICKED EIR boots out over Shika-One, popping a gum bubble, jeans tuned to a soft orange sunrise climbing each thigh in an attempt at levity. It was eir day off, after all. Eir bottom, planted on the cluster's roof edge, was going numb, and a little cold, but e had no intention of moving so e banished it with a shuffle instead. Beside em, Marsh bit eir lip at the city which spread out ahead and around and below. Pod lights winked up and down the neighbouring clusters, an equaliser displaying the rise and fall of Shika-One's life music. Spread out in a non-uniform pattern, the clusters made sure that no one could see to the edge of Hanabi district, no one could see how small their piece of the world was, not even from up here. But Xev knew. They all did. Everyone had walked by the district barriers at some point and wondered what lived in the grey areas of the map.

Filling the upper half of a neighbouring cluster, a plasma-board glowed brilliant white. A figure faded in, immaculate with eir platinum hair and crisp blue suit. Towering over them, it stared out across the cityscape with a smile of parental care that seemed to encompass everyone while looking at none of them.

A voice, friendly cold, pulsed out across the ar-el soundscape. No Access buffs would block this one out. Helpless, Xev and Marsh could do nothing but wait for it to end.

"Hello everyone. My name is Herbert Stanhope, co-founder of the Takano-Stanhope Corporation. Here at TSC Central, we keep the needs of Shika-One at the heart of everything we do. Here, where new synths are born every day, we pride ourselves on giving the human race what it needs to survive."

The figure shrank, pulling to one side, and the background faded in until Stanhope stood beside an immense floating cube which pulsed with light, giving brief glimpses into the corners of a domed room.

"Without the need for wires or interfacing, there's nothing to slow the Euripides, the most advanced artificial intelligence in the world. Originally designed—"

"Why do they keep showing this? Like we don't know?" Marsh interrupted.

"Lest we forget how much we owe them," replied Xev.

"—be used to run this city. This, the cradle of humanity. But, fear not. People are still at the heart of our city. While the Euripides Artificial Intelligence handles the complex calculations that are necessary to automate much of what happens in Shika-One, it's people like you and me who control Euripides."

Stanhope walked from left to right, the background darkening once more to become a vast glowing map of the city. In the foreground, windows slid into view displaying groups of hard-working synths silhouetted against the glow of the Euripides cube, overseeing food cube manufacture, smiling in the glow of surveillance monitors.

"You think Stanhope was a synth?"

"Nah. Eir mummy and daddy made em all sweaty and proper."

Marsh's laugh seemed to banish the gargantuan spirit, as the plasma-board faded to darkness.

"So why am I here with you today?" Stanhope's voice asked.

"You're not! You're long gone, buddy!" Xev shouted out across the chasm.

Marsh's laugh could have rattled the dome.

Stanhope continued, shameless.

"I'm here to tell you about a new initiative. A new idea from TSC, inspired by you, our friends, our family…"

Stanhope faded into view, arms open in an embrace eir children would never feel, the background a soft whiteout.

"How must it be to have your face and voice made a sham?" Marsh asked. "They can make you say anything and you're not even around to say 'no'."

"Creepy, for sure."

A smile spread across Marsh's oblong face.

"Quick, what'll it be? Guess before e says it."

"Um, Miyahara's template to be recalled on account of their stupid pugly faces offending innocent synths!"

Marsh barked a laugh before joining in.

"All Wardens to have smileys painted on their helmets!"

Their time was up.

"—we've taken your feedback about food cubes, Shika-One's most fundamental nutritional source. Their taste, their shape. And we have listened. Now, just for you, our friends, we bring these—" Stanhope's hand unfolded on three sickly pale discs, each the slightest shade different, which expanded and zoomed in until it was all that the synths could see. "—discs. Easier to chew and a more pleasant shape for the mouth. Not only that, but they now come in three flavours: bacon, prawn and lemon."

Now back to that giant, grey-haired and much-tanned face, irises of silver, pupils like great mouths.

"From everyone here at TSC—" the sham CEO gave a conspiratorial wink "—you're welcome."

The screen faded to sleep once more.

"Right," Xev rolled eir eyes. "We killed a synth yesterday, so have some bacon-flavoured, squashed down food cubes."

A black blanket of silence drifted down, strewing its

quiet over the cluster-tops.

"Let's run away," Marsh said, abruptly. "Get right out. All the way."

Xev laid a hand on Marsh's thigh, eir eyes like balls of steel, eir voice breathy.

"You're right, Marsh. Let's run away. We'll steal a cycle and escape. We'll get right out and, in three days, when all our hair has fallen out and the water won't stay in our bellies, we'll die smiling because we're free."

Marsh placed eir own hand on Xev's.

"Let's do it tonight."

There was a silence between them, made deeper by the susurration of the streets below.

Xev snorted a laugh.

"You broke first!" Marsh chuckled.

"Waggling your eyebrows is cheating!"

"I waggled naught. You broke. I win."

They chuckled for a moment, letting the laughter fade though their smiles remained.

"Can you imagine?" Xev said, eir jovial tone settling to some dark amusement. "'Let's run away'. Us, off on some far and away adventure. Not likely."

Marsh nodded. "You feel that sun? Even the little they let through the UV dome for growing cooked that synth in seconds. Get outside the black, then outside the secondary dome, we'd be microwave tofu in a split second."

Xev gave eir friend a weak smile. "Guess we just keep on."

Marsh threw up eir hands and sighed. "Speaking of, where's your new best friend? The one you replaced me with?"

"E's with Tecks, taking the full day to load as much as e can. After the bulletin I could barely get em to move."

"You think e's defective?"

"No way to tell. E never says anything. What say we listen to a little music, then we can log for a few levels of fresh air and bathe in drake blood."

Marsh's eyes lit up. "Drakes?"

"Just this once. And you better heal me if I'm going to be doing all the work again."

Accessing eir auditory cortex, Xev selected one of eir playlists. Tapping each other's nodes, they started the sync.

"You'll like this-is."

The city noise faded, leaving only the dancing lights to accompany a synthesized melody of simple notes over a soft clapping beat.

"What is it with you and this decade?" Marsh asked.

"Shhhh. It was the best-est," Xev replied, as another voice came softly to them, picking up the melody with humble tones.

SCRUNCHING EIR HAIR in a flash of blue, ramming the uniform cap down onto eir head, Xev turned to the new synth, a study in chaos, buttons off kilter to their partnering holes so that the uniform splayed and bunched, its own cap placed atop its head bearing no resemblance to its true function.

"Well, there's effort, at least. Come here."

Without ceremony, Xev began to undress the synth. E couldn't help marvelling just a little at the new body, every freckle and hair, skin like a virgin page. The neat little nipples and dappling of pale hair at the navel. Not a single tattoo or implant, no decoration other than what e was grown with. It was a good template, but Xev thought that of everyone's but eir own. The synth tilted its head. Xev had stared a little too long. Averting eir eyes, e was refastening the last of the synth's buttons when Miyahara burst in, that same old yellow shirt, hair a newly bleached slash atop eir head. Eir hair changed every damned week.

"That thing better do its job today. It's had long enough to learn. If it doesn't, it's your dez on the line," e growled.

Xev kept right on staring at the buttons between eir fingers until Miyahara huffed and slammed eir way back out of the locker room.

"Serious now, you are gonna say something today, right?"

The synth's face stretched from the look of worried bemusement that it usually wore to a faint smile like the first lick of a fire's heat after a walk in the snow. But there was nothing more.

"Too late to worry now." Xev tapped the synth's Access node and had eir own tapped in return. "In the tube with you-ou. Be good-ud."

The synth turned on the spot, looking down at its feet then up at the hole above. With the first jerk of motion, it managed to keep its balance by pressing hands to the walls. E looked back down at Xev for a second before disappearing.

"Please be good," Xev muttered as the ceiling ate the synth.

Taking a seat on the locker room bench, Xev started to Access the Burger Stop's internal cameras, cycling through each image to get to grips with what e could see. Miyahara had given em permission, for the day, to watch the new worker. From the camera's positions above The Burger Stop, it seemed much smaller. The Hanabi lights streamed in through the window, reflecting from the chrome tables and chairs so that they seemed to spin and fluctuate with the pulse of the district. It wasn't busy this morning. There was only the top of a greasy, long-haired head atop leather-clad shoulders at one table, and a crown of brown waves faded through orange to red tips at another.

Little coloured dots, moving on a map, getting smaller and smaller the more you try to see at once, Xev thought. E shook eir head for a second. That was an odd thought, for sure. E was snapped back to the vid-feed by a familiar voice.

"Welcome– to Burger Stop."

Xev shuffled on the bench.

"Alright, here we go. C'mon, coochy."

Through the sync e saw the white fade, the tube slide open, soft light from the synth's uniform and the fair-haired sham laid over the new synth's hairless head.

"C'moooooon," Xev mumbled through gritted teeth to the empty locker room.

"Thank you for choosing Burger Stop. How may I help you today?"

"Yatta!" Throwing up eir arms, Xev almost fell from the bench, but righted emself for the next part.

The synth's delivery was sweet, calm. A little shy. The Access' modulation changed the sound but there was no hiding the delivery. That was eir synth, talking. Xev strained to hear the new sound, to savour it like a sweet treat.

The Corp synth was a biggie. The kind rarely seen in Hanabi. The suit was of particularly fine make with quilted shoulders and a row of little holograms across the left lapel were signs of jobs well done, and lots of xp made.

What's a bigwig like you doing in a place like this? Xev wondered. But it wasn't hard to figure. The belly. E'd come from a neighbouring district for something that e couldn't get back home. A new tonic, perhaps? Or a particular synth in the harems e'd taken a liking to.

Whatever. Just sit and eat your meal all nice.

"Table," the Corp synth demanded, seeming bored by the need to interact.

"Follow me, please."

Yes. Good so far. When the new synth spoke again,

Xev found emself nodding, mouthing along with the Company karaoke:

"Take a seat, if it pleases you. And summon us when you are ready to order. Can I help you further?"

No answer from the Corp type. The new synth turned away, heading back to the tube.

Xev found e was talking to emself.

"Success! That's one down. Now you just have to do it another million times and we're home free—"

A mutter, half heard; a predatory growl from the Corp-type.

"Just had two of you," e said. "But I could always have three. You let me know if you want some real experience."

Xev jerked on the bench.

"Ow! What the—"

A strike, translated through the sync. The Corp suit had hit the new synth. That kisama had struck it right on the behind, hard enough to rattle the synth's knees. Xev could feel the heat spreading across eir skin, the synth would feel it even worse.

In the sync window, the view swung around.

"Wait. No," Xev gasped.

Xev tapped an urgent message through Miyahara's manager feed.

Message: Xev: WALK AWAY.

The feed didn't move. All Xev could see was all the synth saw; the suit, looking up from eir table, a snarl-grin on eir face.

Xev begged the empty room:

"Back to the tube with you. Walk away. Where's Miyahara?"

There e was, at the back of the Burger Stop, slithering in through the rear door.

"Back to the tube, back to the tube!" Xev begged in vain.

A waiting synth bustled past bearing a tray piled with more trays. The new synth selected one from the top, calm as can be.

Xev's breath burnt where e held it.

The Corp synth's satisfied snarl melted, eir eyes widening in a stellar explosion. The tray scythed through the air, smashing eir temple with enough force to send rich red blood spattering across the sterile landscape of the Burger Stop. As e reeled back, shielding eir head with an arm, the tray dropped to the table, a cough of crimson decorating the chrome.

In the crashing echoes of the strike, there was chaos. The leather-clad synth clapped and whooped, the flame-head backing across the room until eir back was against the window, Miyahara shouted and waved eir hand as e Accessed the...the Wardens.

Xev stared at the hole where the tube had disappeared for a second, then hurled emself toward the back door.

"Let me out, let me out damn you!" Accessing the Burger Stop's emergency protocol through Miyahara's borrowed link, Xev punched the fire alarm and the door burst open as e barrelled through. In the Burger Stop camera panel, all synths clapped hands over ears as the sonic beacon pulsed out, shaking the windows in frames and eyeballs in sockets. Through the sync, Xev's ears exploded with the fire beacon in stereo sound, eir own and the synth's, enough to vibrate brains to paste. In the centre of the room, the new synth's feed jerked this way and that, head whipping between faces and the door.

Xev ran-fell up the stairs to the alleyway as the new synth's feed bolted straight for the Burger Stop door. Hitting the street at full tilt, Xev saw it on the threshold, its glowing white uniform a beacon even in the Hanabi lights. Terror washed across the synth's face as, around it, everyone had stopped, were staring their faces pale and eyes sunken in the uniform's glow.

A rumble underfoot, the thud of boots on concrete.

The Wardens' faceless helmets emerged from the crowd. Surrounding.

Xev fought eir way toward the synth, but the massing crowd was too dense. E shoved and pushed and strove but syrup is syrup and e couldn't get through. The synth saw em, its eyes lit with recognition and, in the sync, Xev saw emself struggling to reach shore in a river of people. The new synth's teeth closed, opened, met its lower lip, forming a word unheard.

The sync panel winked out as the news bulletin kicked in.

Xev froze as every pair of eyes widened, pupils dilating to accept the unbidden Access feed. Emself from above, frozen scant meters from eir friend. Wardens, stalking in.

Switch perspective. Through the synth's eyes, petrified, darting, air rasping into its lungs, looking down as red dots lit its chest, hip, leg and arm.

Schracckk.

The synth's body pulsed. Xev rocked at the feel of it. The crowd rose and fell like seaweed caught in a wave. Scarlet filled the air, a festival explosion to rival the Hanabi lights.

Perspective shifted for the replay. From above now, showing the whole of the Burger Stop frontage, the dark pavement, the glowing synth looking not at the Wardens, but off to one side. A word hung in the air and deep red fireflies danced across its body. The Burger Stop façade, painted scarlet as the glowing white uniform was torn asunder.

The bulletin cut. Xev blinked.

Ribbons. Ribbons of a person strewn across the ground.

A Warden stepped forward, stooped, plucked an intact head from the gory ground by an ear, the Access node dangling by its wire from the ravished neck, growing dark, winking out.

Xev retched, eir body rejecting what e'd seen, heard, felt; trying to push it all up and out of eir throat. Through the shivers, the sobs:

"E said my name. E said my name."

Xev blinked hard, shook eir head, tried to clear eir vision, but all e saw was the watery blur of the tyrant Miyahara's yellow shirt, stepping from the Burger Stop's glass frontage sprayed red, a motion of the manager's hand as e looked right at em with that smug pug snarl.

Designation Void

PART II
Void

So many little motes.
Blown back and forth in the vent-draught.
Fallen from destiny's loom to float through
the cosmos.

6

XEV HAD NEVER noticed how warm the Burger Stop had been until e wandered through Hanabi district wearing only eir deactivated uniform and the ineffective slippers designed solely for restaurant tiles. E had managed to keep those by running away when Miyahara not only denied em access to eir own clothing but demanded what e was wearing be returned. Although synths in more revealing outfits moved around em, Xev walked the streets with arms wrapped tight around emself. Anyone could see em now, e knew. Anyone could see that e'd been undezzed. E would be a non-entity in their Access, a huddled and weeping shadow between the glowing masses. In the river of bodies, eyes upon eyes followed em, stripping em bare with their curiosity, fascinated by eir dullness.

With eir Access revoked there were no holo-shams on

the streets or in the windows, no soulless voices on the air. The holo-signs were gone, taking their colours and leaving only the shadow-coated faces of mighty clusters staring down. Perhaps worst of all, Xev could finally see the other synths just as they were, without Access filters adding glam and glitter around faces and outfits. Just base templates with sunless skin and underscored eyes. There was only the cutting breeze of the atmo turbines down the street, the hum of garbage dumpsters and the stomp of thousands of synth feet on bare concrete to listen to.

Xev's body started to jerk and shiver like a tonic addict needing their tubes filled. Wandering past an alley mouth, eir stomach churned.

The image of the new synth's face rose in eir mind. The final look, as eir eyes grew sad, head tilting with that frustrating curiosity, eyebrows slowly lifting as e saw Xev push eir way through the crowd to rescue em. The first splatter of pale blood on eir cheek, face collapsing into confusion, the precursor to pain, and the concussion of rapid fire shaking the flesh on eir bones.

Darting into an alley, Xev dropped to eir knees in the filth and retched. Nothing would come. E knelt there a while longer, body spasming with nothing to show for it but cold spit. Eventually, e made it to eir feet and back out into the crowd, staying close to the walls, away from the buffeting pinball machine of bodies, hugging the cold concrete until e reached home.

Turning on the spot, Xev felt a flutter of panic. This

was where it should be. Where was the rickety old pawn shop? The thrift store? The pulsing pink and cream Lolita haven?

Spinning, hands clenching and unclenching at eir sides, Xev's eye fell on something e recognised. A bicycle, stencilled in red paint above a doorway. The shops were right there. Three doors, all open to the street, but the façades were gone, just Access illusions to make them look old, bright, trendy.

Falling against the rusted grid of the cluster door, Xev waved a hand through the air.

E laughed. E laughed as eir legs gave way and eir bottom hit the step. E laughed as e waved eir hand through the air again and saw nothing but miming fingers. A conductor, lost and alone in the pit. E laughed until chuckles turned to sobs.

7

"Strewth, Xev."

Tecks caught em as Xev fell through the door but, not strong enough to hold eir friend's exhausted weight, they fell to the library's ragged red carpet together.

"Did you see?" Xev spluttered.

Shuffling, Tecks pulled Xev to em, stroking eir hair in waves of electric blue.

"No. Undezzed don't get the mandatory broadcasts. But I heard."

"My Access doesn't work, Tecks. I can't send Marsh a message. I'm cut off. And Miyahara wouldn't let me get my clothes. My pod won't let me in."

"How long have you been wandering the district in this damned uniform?"

The uniform's pristine white plastic was dirtier than it had ever been, the thin material smudged from Xev's wandering. The hat had been lost somewhere in the last few hours.

"I reached the district wall, and then another one. You know, they're just fogged plastic. You can even see people over there, moving around. But they're all blurry and ghostly. It's like the TSC want you to see. Dangling it in front of you so you'll try to earn enough xp to travel there. You think it's just like here, Tecks?" The moment faded to silence when eir friend had no answers to give. Xev eventually sat up, face slashed with tears. "What did you show em, Tecks? The new synth. What could have made em do that?"

Tecks shook eir head and cradled Xev to eir chest. "Nothing that you or I or any other synth hasn't seen. E smacked some suit, right? Killed em dead?"

"No, just hit em."

"Lies travel faster than truth. I think what made em do it was the same as what would make us. E just didn't have the restraint."

"You mean e hadn't had every bit of spark crushed out of em. Like we have."

"Let's get you off the floor. If anyone walks through that door, the way you're laid they'll see everything you've got."

"I don't care. Let them see. I'll be harem meat by tomorrow anyway."

"No, you won't, little cutlet. I won't let you."

WHEN THE SHIVERING had stopped thanks to an old blanket and a hot mug held like a lifeline between eir hands, Xev sniffed one last time, wiped eir nose on a naked wrist, and finally looked up from where eir bare feet made fists on the concrete floor of Tecks' library alcove. The shoes had gone too. Where and when, e had no clue. Perhaps living on the run with the hat, somewhere.

Hard at work, Tecks was managing to run five synth feeds while reprogramming Xev's.

The librarian's chair swung around.

"Alright. We can get you connected on the subnet for messaging but, as you know, that's about it. Anything bigger and the Corp would likely decide not to ignore us hijacking their transmitters. I've managed to recover your xp total through a back door. You can top it up with the game, at least, but you'll need to play hardcore from now on if you want to stay floaty."

"Not important." Xev mumbled.

"Unless you start mixing tonics or pushing your plums, there'll be no food for you. You need to eat. Need to sleep. The game's where you'll have to go if you want to stay legit."

"I've never been any good at it. I'll have to live here. On this stool. I'll be a parrot."

"We'll need to programme your hair optics more colours."

Xev made the sound of a chuckle and gave a smile that didn't reach further than eir mouth.

"Did you get Marsh?"

"E's coming through when e gets off shift. Back to the matter at hand. What do you want to do now you're undezzed?"

"I don't know. I can't think."

Tecks nodded. "Fair."

Xev felt eir face contract, scrunch like a paper cup. It was coming again.

"They shredded em, Tecks. Took what was left and tossed em in the shredder. Put eir head in a box and—" with a squeak as eir throat tightened, the rest was lost to tears and tears and tears.

Eir chair rattling forward on old wheels, Tecks put aside Xev's mug and leant awkwardly to hug em again. "Sure. Try not to think on it. I'm the only one who can replay things, you got it?"

MERCIFULLY, MARSH BROUGHT shoes and a wardrobe of cast-offs that, with a few ties and tugs, managed to look surprisingly Belly-fashionable. Still, Xev sat regarding eir feet rather than eir friend across one of the mismatched library tables.

"How're you doing over there?" asked Marsh.

Gently raking eir hair forward, making it a curtain to hide behind, Xev muttered, "Examining my existence with a microscope."

"That way lays danger."

"I need xp. And I'm not cut out for illegality, Marsh.

I'm not streetwise or clued in. I've never taken a tonic in my life. I've never even played a dodgy module."

"You're a squeaky clean one, that's for sure."

"And I suppose you're a rogue?"

Marsh winked. "I get around."

Xev gave a disbelieving snort. They sat quiet for a while with Marsh scrutinising eir friend for any sign of revelation or recovery and Xev's blankness avoiding all detection.

"Let's go," Marsh demanded, swooping to eir feet.

Xev startled at the movement, but didn't respond.

"C'mon. Up with you. We've got someone to see."

"Who?"

"Less of that. Up."

"You're being mean."

"I love you," Marsh said, matter-of-fact, and coupled it with a shrug. "C'mon."

Xev curled emself smaller.

"I can't, Marsh. Just let me stew."

"I'm not going to let you turn into a soggy dumpling. If I have to piggy you, I'll do it."

The little grey circles in Xev's eyes rolled up toward Marsh.

"Oink."

Instead, Marsh slung em over eir shoulders like a giant, limp noodle. They made it all the way to the door before Xev slapped Marsh on the back and demanded to be put down.

"Strewth, you're a nuisance. Just let me rot in peace."

"Nope," Marsh said, and ducked through the library doorway, leaving Xev no choice but to follow.

The library was pretty near the belly's edge, on an outstretched limb of alleyways that they now followed further in. Deeper. Without eir Access providing the yellow outlines of people and things, the experience was an odd one. Shapes moved indistinct in the dark, voices lanced out without warning or the Access regulating volume. Xev scampered behind Marsh, jerking eir head this way and that, startling at every sound and movement, an old synth made to feel naked-new. As they went deeper, the press of bodies became a swarm. As the crowd grew thicker, Xev rocked in the flow of synths, lost if it weren't for Marsh's wayfaring.

And in that crowd, faces. Without Access shams, Xev saw emself everywhere. Em with green lips and hair, em with a glowing tonic tube haloing eir throat, two of em lost in lust for everyone to witness. Every kind of em. But that wasn't so bad. It was the others. The new synth's template was there, too. Older, of course, with hair and clothes bought after their naming; studs in ears and brows, fingertips painted or irises artificially coloured. But Xev's shredded friend was there, in them all, and every flash of that face brought the slack-jawed, neckless head to mind. Eyes open and they were there, eyes closed was no better. Grabbing the back of Marsh's jacket, grinding eir teeth against the faces, the memories, Xev focussed on the ground and let emself be led.

COMING TO AN open space made by a junction of three alleys, Xev was forced to look up when someone called eir name. The synth stepped out from under a pulsing red neon "X", moving away from two others of the same template, their hair cut into the same asymmetric bob, trousers and jackets cheap and matching. Everything about them fought the synth urge to be individual, to modify emselves. Xev couldn't help but notice that the synth's collarbone tattoo had been removed. Eir stomach lurched.

"Xev. Hi." The voice wasn't one Xev recognised; the template had been samed beyond any recognition, but e only knew one synth personally with that face.

"Toriq?"

"Yeah." The word hung on an exhalation, as if said by accident. There was a smile that seemed to come from far away, perhaps the same distant place that Toriq's eyes were focussed. Those eyes, tinged with green veins. "Yeah, Xev. How long has it been? Too, too long."

"A few weeks. It's been just a few weeks."

As Toriq reached out for em, Marsh intervened.

"Real good to see you, for sure. You best get back to your pals. Someone over there's looking stormy."

That seemed to snap Toriq to attention, eir head whipping around to regard a glaring synth who had stepped out of the shadows beneath the red X and between the other members of the perfectly-matched trio. There was indeed a thunderous look there.

Toriq wandered back, without a word.

Xev buried eir face in eir hands. "Oh no, Marsh. Oh no, oh no…"

"Hey, that ain't you. On we go," and e half-dragged eir friend away.

WHERE A RHYTHMIC light pulsed at the other side of the area, Marsh led them through one doorway, then another, squeezing past synths in corridors plastered with paper fliers faded beyond reading. Through that way, they stepped out onto a steel balcony overlooking a mass of bodies below. Arms and legs and heads and hips going through every motion of dance, embracing, back to back, side to side. But the only sounds were the shuffling of feet, the hush of clothing on clothing, the odd snatch of conversation. They were all synced, each group or couple Accessing their own song that they might dance alone despite the crowd.

This was what it was like to spend xp on something other than food. Xev had felt this before in Tecks' old movies. In those records of a lost age, when the sun was still a life-giver and not a scorching, spiteful orb, Xev had seen open beaches, sighing forests, and long stretches of desert road. And the same feeling came to em now as e looked around, a feeling that e had no word for. There was liberty in the air, Xev could feel it somewhere down in eir

DNA, crying out for a thing e had never tasted.

"Here, I'll play us something." Marsh Accessed one of eir personal playlists and they synced.

Something like a heartbeat entered Xev's limbic system in perfect, patient time. False, but more real than Xev's own heart. It was hard not to let emself be slowed by it, stabilised. E could feel the continuing certainty of it, and the daunting stroke of a piano over a steel melody made it all the more inevitable. And the movement of the synths below suddenly made more sense.

Xev looked to eir friend, who must have known exactly what e needed to hear.

"There is good music beyond the decade you're obsessed with," Marsh said with a wink.

Below and off to one side, light came in streams through a perforated steel sheet which served as the front of a bar backed by dark bottles with paper labels in row upon row. They headed that way, down the balcony's steel steps as Marsh's music swelled. Xev could feel eir shoulders driven by it, feel emself being lost in the rhythm of primordial atoms, until a crystal-clear voice came to bring em back, to ground em in human concerns such as sadness and fickle certainty. As they moved through the crowd, jostled by dancers who moved too quickly and disjointed for what e was listening to, Xev was certain that this song was about everything e had ever felt, and everything e *was* feeling; the start and the end of all things, of em in the sac where e was grown and the end that e would meet while the universe span on. All at once.

E tapped Marsh on the shoulder as they cut their way through the crowd.

"I need this song," e said, perhaps a little too loud.

An unknown synth they passed close by gave em a knowing smile, a nod that sent hair cascading down a pretty face. Xev's own face flushed.

Marsh grinned. "Hang out here, be-ar-be."

E left for the bar, leaving Xev alone.

Turning on the spot, the song still tingling through eir mind, Xev came face to face with the smiling synth.

"What're you listening to?"

Xev gulped. A slash of red/orange gradient makeup across eir eyes, hair a blonde waterfall over one shoulder of a sea-green rayon shirt, e was striking enough to halt any attempts at answering.

The synth smiled, lifted a hand as e said, "You mind?"

Xev shook eir head and felt the synth's fingers on eir neck, joining the sync. Instantly, the stranger began to move to the slower beat.

"This is good," e said, nodding to it.

The synth's arms moved around Xev's waist, that blonde torrent close enough to smell a pleasant perfume-less clean, and Xev was embracing a stranger.

"You've been crying," the synth said. Xev didn't answer but clung on as they swayed together. "It'll be ok. You know?"

And they danced for a while, turning cosmic slow to

the music.

As soon as Xev made to pull away, the synth let it happen.

"I better go find my friend."

"Sure. Thanks for the song."

The synth turned away, still dancing to the slower beat that Xev could now feel from toes to teeth.

When Xev made it up to the bar, Marsh was half way through one of the brown bottles. E gave Xev the other half with an I-saw-that smile and stood with em as the song faded.

8

A DOOR BEHIND the speakeasy's bar led to a corridor with intermittent leather pads on the walls, low-lit with soft-glow light strips at floor level. Halfway, a synth in black velveteen, a slash of flesh on view from collar to navel, languished against a wall with no seeming desire to be in the bar or whatever room lay beyond the red door at the corridor's end. Marsh gave the synth an unreciprocated nod as they passed.

"Paizo can help. I told em all about you while you were shaking booties with your new friend."

"Hush, will you? It was just a dance."

"A dance is never just a dance. Therapy, love, release, but never *just* a dance."

"You stole that from somewhere."

"Probably a film."

The red door concealed a sumptuous lounge, lit so

that the ceiling could have been a foot away or somewhere in infinity. Ribs of scarlet cloth swooped from the darkness above to a carpeted floor where chaises were scattered haphazardly. From one of these, with its back to the door, an elegant arm dappled in dark hair stretched, beckoned.

Xev looked to eir friend who shooed em across the room.

Taking a circuitous route, Xev crept forward until the reclining figure came into view. In the same deep red as the door, the walls, the upholstered chaise, the synth's clothes were loose, almost draughty, sharing a tantalising view of a dark-haired chest from beneath a half-kimono pant suit. Eir hair, impeccably piled atop a statuesque head and leading down to laser-accurate stubble, was metallic black. Xev missed a beat. While e had seen the template before, in shops and bars, on streets and balconies, e had never seen it so perfectly put together.

The synth spoke with sensuous certainty. "Seat yourself," and the order went direct-line to Xev's legs, eir bottom hitting a chaise opposite. "Marshy says you've had a bad day, little one."

Marsh cut in, from the door. "E could really use somewhere to stay, Paizo—"

A fast tick escaped Paizo's pursed lips.

Tut-tut.

"Sorry," Marsh mumbled.

Xev swallowed before speaking.

"E's right. I need somewhere to go."

"Too easy, too easy," Paizo groaned with a wave of a hand. Eir tone changed from bored to a seriousness bordering on predatory. "Give me a challenge."

"Somewhere that doesn't smell like wet mould and for no xp at all?"

Paizo's laugh came in a clear ring. Eir teeth were *perfect*.

Is it even possible to have sexy teeth? Xev thought.

"I'll see what I can do. Marshy, don't you have somewhere to be?"

Marsh's focus drifted for a second as e checked eir Access.

"I have a few more hours before I really need to sleep."

"No, Marsh, go home. You've done enough. Don't be so tired that you lose your own dez. You're the respectable one now." Xev forced a smile.

Marsh squinted at em. "That ain't ever gonna be so. But maybe I should go. Paizo?"

The reclining synth waved a dismissive hand. "No fear."

Reluctantly, Marsh turned away, keeping eyes on Xev as long as e could before stepping out.

Paizo typed mid-air, sending some message or other. A moment later, the velveteen hallway synth stepped in. The way e moved, eir shoulders and hips were never straight, always sloping one way or the other, always lounging even when stood in the middle of a room.

"Dathice, my little cooch, take our new friend to eir place of dwelling."

Xev stood to follow as Dathice turned to leave without even looking eir way.

"What about the xp?"

"Ten percent," Paizo was bored again.

"Of?"

"Everything." Paizo fixed em with eir gaze, eyes filled with threat or offer – it was hard to tell. Something in Xev's lower stomach flipped, but e couldn't figure if it was fear or attraction. "And there better be something."

Xev nodded and followed Dathice out through the red-panelled corridor.

Back through the darkened crush of synths, Xev scanned for eir dancing partner without realising it, and they soon stepped back out into the belly. Along an alley not too far from the speakeasy, Dathice led Xev to a cluster unlike any other. Xev had never been this deep into the belly, this far from Hanabi's light-dance, and had no idea these pseudo clusters were even here. But here they were, several of them, half-sized and blank faced but definitely clusters of a kind. Inside, and up a square spiral of stairs, Dathice motioned to a grimy steel doorway, letting Xev open it before leading the way. Xev looked at eir dirt-stained hand as they walked on. The sly cooch hadn't wanted dirty hands.

On through another corridor and another flick of the chin from Dathice. Xev opened a metal door to reveal, rudimentary but unmistakable, a pod. A little box, lit around the floor, a low shelf its only feature, a handle stuck out from beneath. A pillow-less, anaemic mattress on top.

"Cosy," Xev offered.

Without ceremony, Dathice reached for Xev's neck. E flinched away, but the velveteen synth didn't waver. An odd sync kicked in. No sight or sound, just small red numbers appearing beside Xev's xp total.

10%

And Dathice was gone, a whiff of weak perfume in the bleak air, the slam of eir heeled boot on the rusted door echoing back down the hall.

Alone in eir (pod seemed wrong, now) cube, Xev checked the sub-bed drawer and found it empty, then laid on the inch-thin mattress and shuffled into something resembling comfort. It was wider than the one in eir old pod. Apparently, the builders of this old haunt had no problems with synths sharing. Eir xp would hold for today, maybe even a few if e didn't buy new clothes. Plus, gaming tired was never a good idea. If e was scrapped in-game as well, e'd have nothing left. E Accessed one of the few menus left to em, the auditory cortex storage.

"Can't take this from me."

A sound that e'd never heard ar-el began to tinkle down into Xev's mind. Rainfall. A safe, repetitive tympanum coaxed a sorrowful synthesizer for the faceless, mournful voice to lullaby over. Laying back eir head, e let the music wash away the calamity of the day, or at least give em something to fall asleep to.

It was only partially successful on both counts.

9

MARSH ARRIVED TO find Xev cross-legged in the corridor outside eir cube, facing the door.

"Up to something, rebel?"

Xev turned, revealing the multi-tone pot in eir lap, a plastic bristled paintbrush in hand, and the mural that now decorated the door. In a t-shirt cut to sit off the shoulder and tatty denim, eyes heavily darkened with punches of pink around them, e looked every bit the belly synth e'd become in just a few short weeks.

Marsh's jaw dropped at the transformation, but e held back comment.

"I'm nearly done. Hold on," Xev said, and popped eir bubblegum.

Marsh leant against the tiny sliver of wall that separated each cube, shuddering in the emotionless concrete corridor, and watched. It didn't take long for Xev to sit back. The design was angular, heavily stylised, but depicted a rooster feather from red base through purple to a green tip. Xev twisted the multi-tone pot's bottom and the liquid inside faded from green to clear.

"Not bad," Marsh offered.

"Didn't feel like home without it."

"Where'd you get the toner?"

"Borrowed it in exchange for a song."

"Quite the business-person. Let's get inside. I need to let off some steam."

Getting themselves comfortable side-by-side on the bed shelf, Marsh muttered: "Well this is just cosy as."

"Say, you been around the Burger Stop?" Xev asked, careful to maintain a barely interested tone.

"Sure," Marsh said, a tinge of uncertainty in eir voice.

Xev left it quiet for a beat. Marsh lifted emself onto one elbow to regard eir friend steadily.

"Thought just ran across me, is all," Xev lied as e stared at the lifeless grey rectangle of the ceiling. "Just a little wonder. Never mind."

"Don't be looking back, now. They sure won't be," Marsh added softly. "And don't be going back, neither. They'd sic the Wardens on you, you better believe. There's naught to be done."

"For sure. Just seems all it takes is a new sham to forget someone."

"You got too much thinking time on your hands," Marsh said, lying back and shuffling into a comfortable position to log.

"That's the thing," Xev sighed. "Stood in that tube, I always did have the time, but I never used it. Now, everything's different. The walls are gone. I can expand. It's scary out here, Marsh."

Marsh's hand found Xev's and gave a little squeeze.

"Hey, now. Don't go getting weird on me. Weirder, anyways." E winked. "Too much thinking—"

"Thinking's all there is. Without the shams and the noise. Makes me wonder the whys, you know?"

Marsh gave em a worried look from the corner of eir eye.

"Some fun is needed right now, methinks. Your brain needs a break. So, let's break something."

As they lay back and prepared to enter the menu space, Marsh waited for Xev's eyes to lose focus, then jabbed eirs right in the ribs with a sharp finger. Xev had just enough time to feel it, but not enough to react, as e entered the free-float on way to the Alkia module.

Bouncing on mechanical knees, Xev took in Alkia's verdant green intro area. E moved around, not cherishing the view as e once had, before e had to spend more and more time in the module making xp to eat and pay off Paizo. Drawing back one mechanical hand, grinding closed eir iron fist, e waited. Seconds later, Marsh's avi wafted into existence, and Xev released the punch. Marsh folded in two, blown back off eir feet, and hit the grass a distance away. With a warning trill, Xev's Access flashed a red message.

> WARNING: PvP combat in the intro area is heavily discouraged

As punishment, eir hp halo fell from green to amber, exactly half, as in the distance Marsh's bar refilled.

"That wasn't very nice," Marsh's voice sighed over the team chat channel.

"You deserved it," Xev chuckled.

As Marsh sauntered back toward em, leather cloak billowing, e paused for a second as e regarded Xev's readout.

"Three weeks. You've had no dez for three weeks and you're a level higher than me." Marsh's avi voice turned the complaint into something akin to a song. E shook eir platinum hair, eir pointed ears twitching with frustration.

Xev's own avi looked down at eir friend with a creak of metal.

"I have nothing else to do, no other way to make xp. I can't help but level. And if I start a new module alone, the lower levels won't keep me in Paizo's good graces."

Marsh humphed, or tried. Eir avi didn't humph well and it came out in a melodious hum.

"You can make it up to me. We're going treasure hunting. I need a new focus." Marsh lifted eir current magical focus, a red gem that fit in eir palm. "I know just the quest."

There was no argument from Xev, and Marsh didn't give em time to in any case. Eir gem pulsed with light, and e blurred into motion, darting ahead under a speed spell. Xev broke into a run, eir much longer legs and tireless mechanical build covering the ground with ease. The air before them became a circular blur, a portal *in potentia*, maintaining its distance even as they ran. Marsh Accessed the right quest and the blur rushed forward, claiming them.

THE GROUND TURNED from grass to gravel.

A volcanic wasteland filled the valley before them, gouts of syrupy lava spewing up from beneath the earth to sizzle and settle. Xev swore e could feel eir metal skin prickle with whatever the Forged version of sweat was.

"The plot?"

Marsh's voice took on the tone Xev noticed as eir quoting voice:

"Legend says that salamanders from the fire plane are nesting in a ruined wizard's tower who once used the lava to forge magical artefacts. Legend says—"

"Legend has a lot to say for itself."

"Cool stuff," Marsh sighed. "We're gonna fight things and get cool stuff."

"My motivation?" Xev rumbled.

"Friendship."

Xev's living iron mask raised an eyebrow.

"Shut up. It's xp in the bank for you."

As they descended the slope, heat emanated from both the ground and the air, coming in even stronger waves when geysers of lava burst from the earth in glowing plumes. In Xev's view, eir Watchful Warrior skill scanned ahead for movement. A seismic rumble forced them to stop dead in order to keep their footing. On the slopes leading down to the ash and shale wasteland, pebbles scuttled and fell.

"Intrigue upon intrigue," Xev rumbled.

Marsh looked to em with an excited grin plastered on eir face.

"Right?" E said, eir voice giddy.

In Xev's view, three pale blue circles zeroed in on unassuming patches of darkness. E extended one long arm with a whir of servos.

"Movement."

As if summoned by the word, deep red shapes moved against the charcoal grey landscape.

"You think they spotted us?" Xev asked, and looked to Marsh, who was turning more transparent by the second.

"Spotted *you*, you mean." And e was gone.

"Hate you, Marsh."

Somewhere to eir right, Xev heard eir friend, stealthily moving away. "Lies."

With a sigh and the long, slow, grind of steel on steel, Xev drew the greatsword from eir back.

The salamanders advanced at full tilt. And, as Xev watched, more and more came shuffle-burrowing out of the ash and shale ground. Lizard-like, scuttling, a faint orange glow leaked from between the armoured plates on their backs.

Using the Access' in-game interface, Xev selected the Hunter's Wisdom skill from the glowing sigils at the corner of eir eye, and was shown possible target areas on the nearest salamander in little green pinpoints. Between the plates, the soft belly.

Sprinting into range, the hissing salamander bunched its body and leapt. With a rapid sidestep, heavy metal feet piling heaps of shale, Xev purposefully missed with eir greatsword, rolling eir armoured shoulder to connect with the salamander, knocking it out of its leap and to the ground. Stepping over it, e carried through the spin, sword orbiting eir body, and slammed the blade through the salamander's exposed stomach. A screech from the creature, and then no movement at all as glowing orange blood oozed from the shattered creature.

CRITICAL HIT

Xev's iron face stretched into a grin. E span in time to catch another beast mid-air and spotted yet another going for eir legs. With the flat of eir blade, e batted the first to the ground, slamming a foot down on the neck of the other. With a jab and twist the crushed creature perished, an arc of splattering orange flicking out across the dust-laden air as Xev's greatsword made a lumberjack swing to cleave the other where it had landed.

The fight devolved into a free-for-all. There were too many in the advancing group now, swarming, that any fancy moves were rendered useless. Xev stepped back as the salamanders bashed against em, chopping furiously with more attacks hitting armoured hide than fleshy belly. Their bites began to hit home, hyper-heated teeth making sizzling indentations in Xev's armour. More came, the weight making Xev's strength stat pulse. E realised that e would be overrun and felt a sob rise in eir throat. If this was it, eir xp would be gone. No cube, no food, and Paizo would likely take eir ten percent out of Xev's ar-el, far more vulnerable, hide.

With three rattling concussions, the centre of the salamander wave erupted. Scaly bodies became smoking chunks that splatted across distant grey dunes. Above them, flickering into view as one spell replaced the other, floated Marsh, eir leather outfit and platinum braid whipping in the volcanic wind, the glow of eir crystal focus fading after the last blast.

Xev felt the wave abate, enough for a shove. Activating Furious Might, e slammed eir shoulder into the rising wave, toppling the salamanders back over themselves, creating a carpet of writhing bellies. Golf swings with eir giant blade sprayed glowing ichor as, above, Marsh pummelled the squirming ground with pulses of arcane energy. E must have activated a skill, because eir avi's animation took over, making complex signals with eir hands, the sound of eir arcane-infused song coming clear over the sounds of battle. Xev dove for cover, throwing arms over helm as the sky broke open, pouring clouds from a celestial fissure, and glowing, purple meteors slammed into the earth, spraying shale and ash and boiling orange blood.

The taste of ash in eir mouth, metallic skin sizzling with evaporating salamander blood, Xev checked eir hp readout. Dark, reddish amber. A winking message appeared beside the readout as Marsh descended from the ash cloud, hands glowing a pale light.

`A teammate is healing you`

As the ash and dust settled around em, Marsh chuckled.

"I told you this would be fun."

10

L EANING OVER THE balcony's rail, Xev sipped coffee that looked, smelled and coated eir insides like liquid latex while e watched the synths below. Unlike the streets of Hanabi where the synths moved in one direction or the other, wherever the streets led, here they were parking lot leaves, wind-tossed in all directions. Colour, greasy leather and sequins blurred together in the gloom only to split apart with a shiver and a rip like bacteria on the spread. And still, for all the textures and styles, the directions taken and decisions made every second to stir the pot, Xev couldn't help but notice the recurring templates: the entire city a living mah-jong.

Of those templates, one still stood out; a face impossibly animated although Xev had seen it die, seen its blood decorate a Burger Stop window. Yet there they all walked. Hundreds of dead faces. Only Xev saw blood soaking through the ar-el makeup and glam.

With a sigh to settle eir roiling mind, e dropped what remained of eir coffee from the balcony to a dumpster below and took the metal steps down to swim through the rainbow oil of belly synths.

DOWN THE PAPER-PLASTERED throat of Paizo's speakeasy, Xev stepped into the dancehall where neon stalactites hung in the darkness above a rapt audience. At the end of the hall a stage had been ushered out of hiding, black as its surroundings so that the synth who stood there seemed to float in the light that reflected from eir silver and black clothing. The Beam, chief of ceremonies.

"Last of all, though not the least, safe from the shred and with a new name new-chosen—" The Beam threw out an arm in summons as the crowd broke into applause. Another synth joined the stage, deathly pale, eyes squinting under the burning attention. What hair e had was still growing through, although there were signs of experimentation with some kind of style. Eir clothes were thrifty but e obviously had a dez with enough xp to spare for a sham-gem bracelet. The Beam held a silver pen aloft and the crowd hushed. Turning to face the newly-named synth so that e was blocked from view, Xev could hear the Beam's pen cut across the silence with a thin *brip-bridiptip*. The newer synth winced, sucking air through eir teeth as The Beam worked. With a flourish, the chief of ceremonies regarded the crowd, eir voice falling like piano notes in the dark.

"My fellow synths. May I introduce... Dino!" The Beam danced aside to reveal the newly named Dino, blinking back tears from the burning of the glyph tattoo that now decorated eir collarbone.

The crowd erupted in a roar of applause and whistles. There must have been a room-sync in place, because lots of bodies began to bounce and sing in unison. Xev didn't feel much like joining. For every synth who made their name, e couldn't help but think about one who hadn't. Instead, e made eir way to the bar and ordered a drink in a small glass. The higher levels of Alkia were paying eir tab tonight.

At the side of eir vision, an Access panel opened so unexpectedly that e startled, almost fumbling eir drink.

Sync invite: Vee-Tee

Scanning the bar, Xev couldn't see a style configuration that e recognised.

Curious, e swiped to accept.

A drumsticks-on-plastic solo popped into Xev's head, followed by a bassline that could have been string, could have been keys. E couldn't help but get into it, tapping eir hand on the bar as e searched for the phantom inviter. As the vocals came in with an innocent voice filled with words of extraordinary experience, Xev saw em. The smiling synth from eir first visit to the speakeasy. The familiar wave of lopsided blonde was now tipped with pale green, and e wore short cropped off-the-shoulder fish scales over leatherette. In half-dancing steps, Vee-Tee made eir way over. Xev forgot eir drink entirely and suddenly they were dancing together as if they had been for hours, days, a lifetime. Xev felt a smile creep across eir face, genuine and alien. The song progressed without building, as if it might drive them on forever, hanging in the crystalline moment of the sync. As if agreeing, the song didn't end, but faded into a lingering promise.

"How did you know—"

"What you'd like?" Vee-Tee interrupted. "Saw your friend with the red bouf and traded em a drink for intel. I know someone who does good work from that decade."

"Fool you," Xev laughed. "E'd have given it up without the beer just to hook us up."

"Are we hooking up?" Vee's mouth twitched a smile that sent blood rushing to Xev's face.

"E's just a bit obsessed with that stuff."

Vee shrugged. "Worth it?"

Xev ran fingers through eir hair with a shimmer of blue. "To me? Sure."

"Wanna get lost?" Vee laid a smile on em like something Xev had only ever felt in-game: perfect beach-day sunshine.

Xev looked toward the door, partly for Marsh, partly longing to go along with whatever Vee-Tee had in mind.

"I'm meeting your co-conspirator. But I have your contact now."

With a shake of eir head, Vee-Tee dispelled any of Xev's remaining illusions. "E ain't coming, pretty cooch. We conspired on that one thing more." Vee-Tee's fingers found Xev's and they knotted together with only the slightest pressure. "I have something for you to see."

Xev let emself be led out of the speakeasy, out to the street, and all the while Vee-Tee seemed to shrug off the seeping grey atmosphere of the belly; the incessant night of Shika-One. Red lights and shadows were nothing to this sleek koi, this liquid creature that drew Xev on into the night. E lost all eyes for landmarks or signs, nothing seemed more of import than Vee-Tee's shimmering form.

Arriving at a doorway outlined with glowing green strip lights, Vee-Tee pulled Xev in tight, performing a neat spin that pressed them together as they passed through the narrow compartment of a revolving door. Xev caught a whisper of hand movement as Vee Accessed their way in.

"It foxes the lock," e said, as e lingered just a second longer than necessary before stepping back from Xev. "Gets us two where only one should go."

Xev looked around, eir jaw dropping at the cluster's interior; a vast space bathed in a source-less white glow. Through the sync, Xev's Access showed holo-panels hung in mid-air at regular intervals, stretching from floor to ceiling. Each showed a map, e supposed, of the cluster's interior, level upon level.

"You're not undezzed," Xev realised. "Your Access still works."

"That's right. This is my dez," Vee offered.

Xev couldn't help but wonder what kind of official designation would be hidden away in the belly. Sure, the Wardens were famous for looking the other way when it came to any activities in the belly that kept the undezzed unshreddables off the main streets. But having an official building buried back here, that just didn't seem right.

They entered a similarly glowing elevator and Vee Accessed a much higher floor. Xev couldn't help but shake eir head.

"I shouldn't be here, Vee. You could lose your dez."

"You'd take me in, wouldn't you?" Vee's eyes showed something that Xev struggled to read, somewhere between playing and pleading.

"Let's hope it doesn't come to that."

"If there's worrying to be done, think like this: either they don't want you here and we're already discovered, or they don't care and all's well."

At that, the elevator door hushed open and Vee advanced into darkness, moving as if it were only a different pool of the same water e'd propelled them through all along.

Somewhere between a minute and a week passed as they walked past low rectangular objects which reminded Xev of in-game quest reward chests. Vee Accessed a small lamp that gave off a diffused amber glow, revealing one of the shapes to be a hip-high plinth. The plinth slid open where there had been no seams only moments before, and a platform rose from inside, tilting as it reached chest height, bringing its load toward them so they might inspect it.

"That can't be real," Xev breathed.

"As real as you or I."

Xev's hand still in eirs, Vee reached out toward a book, heavy bound in functional brown leather. A green band of light caressed their skin and Xev felt an odd tingle. Eir hand was suddenly dry and hot, like the sensation of swift sunburn e'd felt through the bulletin feed.

"It cleans your hands, that's all. Gentle now."

Vee opened the book's crackling cover to reveal even more wonders inside. Page upon page of string bands into which had been slotted dried specimens of a lost world. With delicate deftness, Vee selected one pressed flower from hundreds; a faded violet.

"At the end of the old world, they didn't have a way to preserve what they had, so they dried and pressed things between the pages of books. Can you believe it? Every day, I check through the catalogues and make sure they're all safe in their little rows. Pretty, ain't they?"

Vee offered the flower to em but, when Xev reached out, eir hands shook far too much to be handling something so delicate.

"I can't, my hands."

"Shhhh. It's ok." Vee took Xev's hand, turning it palm up and laid the flower there.

It could have been the anti-bio filter or the alcohol e'd

just drank, but Xev could feel the flower, as weightless as it was, with the same electric sensation as the contact of the synth's hand that lay underneath.

"It makes me sad," Xev sighed.

"How so?"

"Keeping it like this. All dried up and frail."

"Grieving for something you've never known. That's a strange thing."

"I don't see that it is," Xev said. "Don't look at me like a kook."

"That wasn't the look at all. Tell me." Vee took the flower with what seemed like callousness to Xev, returning it to the book and the display to the plinth. Soon there was only them and the light of the lamp. Something about their little amber bubble made Xev feel safer, cut off, preserved from prying eyes. Enough to say what was on eir mind.

"We're trapped in the dirt like some time capsule, only there's no one to find us." Xev brushed the palm of eir flower hand with the fingertips of the other, just in case there was something left to feel. E finally stopped staring at eir hand, turning eir eyes toward Vee's patient smile. "We've been left behind like an old-timey headstone, just to show that the human race was once here. We replay the same days with the same faces, more like a recording than a life. And the synths out there just sit like shams on the merry-go-round, letting it happen as long as everything keeps spinning and the ones who fall off are someone else." Xev made it all the way until that point without eir voice breaking, but eir next words came forced through tightened vocal chords. "It all makes me so sad."

"Pretty cooch, you think too hard." With hands cupping Xev's downturned head, Vee kissed eir forehead as if to ease the frayed mind inside. "Sorry I made you sad."

Looking up at Vee seemed the hardest thing e could ever do, and so Xev simply moved closer, resting eir head on the synth's bare shoulder.

"Think I'm just sad. I just want someone to find a way for us all to move on, Vee."

11

A STRIKE – like being hit with a concrete block – and Xev's armoured body smashed into the cave wall. The hp ring in eir vision pulsed rhythmic red, fading to purple at the edges. It drew in, tunnelling Xev's vision, covering the skills icons that were no longer available in eir damaged state.

The Troll King stretched its neck and rolled its shoulders, milky saliva dripping from its tusks. It snorted, tasting the defeat of its quarry, savouring it.

That's some mighty fine programming, Xev thought as e gritted eir teeth.

The creature's muscles bunched beneath green skin, and it threw itself toward em.

YOU DIED

A flash of red faded to white as Xev fell from the Alkia

module into the free-form float of the menu space. That was a stupid mistake. Letting the Troll King get eir scent in the tunnels was a rookie move. Sloppy. Good job e'd paid xp for a bank slot the previous week and stowed some xp, because e'd just lost more than e'd gained that day. That had made Marsh jealous. Casual gamers with designations didn't have time to earn bank slots.

Floating in the crystal white limbo of the menu space, Xev thought of how little xp e'd made in the last two days. It was getting harder and harder to concentrate and playing such high levels needed real focus.

Logging out, the menu space faded into ar-el as Xev sat up. Accessing eir contacts, e scrolled down to Marsh, hovered, scrolled down to Vee-Tee, and swiped it closed again. Xev shifted to sit on the edge of the cube's bunk, leaning eir elbows on eir knees and resting eir face in eir hands. After a moment, e began to massage eir chest, just under eir heart where a hot little fist clenched right in the centre of em. Like fear, it fluttered and stole eir breath. Unlike fear, it didn't pass. No matter what e did, it remained. Xev felt a pinprick of cold on eir knee and opened eir eyes in time to see the tear make its sliding journey down eir naked calf to the floor.

"Not again," e muttered, and squeezed eir eyes closed. These tears came too frequently, now. Unbidden and often caused by nothing at all. Xev tried to breathe but there was something stuck inside em. E felt twisted like a wrung rag. The bare cube pressed in on every side, made even smaller by piles of empty food packs in one corner and a pile of dirty clothing ready for the laundro-vac in the other. The walls pressed against eir temples. The air, usually cool in the concrete space, felt syrupy in eir lungs.

Xev jarred when eir bottom hit the corridor floor. E was shivering, still dressed only in the vest and pants e'd been gaming in. The cube's door lay open, the light still on inside, but e couldn't remember clearing the intervening space. That feeling in eir chest thrummed like an atmo-turbine. Eir palms were sweaty, eir head pounded. A sense of primal urgency flooded eir system as if the Troll King had followed em into ar-el to continue its attack.

Another pulse of fearful tension. This time, Xev had a little thought left. E darted toward the cube, grabbed whatever clothes e could from the dirty pile, and ran at full tilt toward the stairs. In another disjointed blink, e was out into the street, clutching leather-reinforced jeans and a ragged, cropped tee to eir chest as faces swam and loomed in the dark around em.

E ran, half stumbling, bouncing from people and dumpsters, through the belly, still holding eir clothes, until e reached the hand-painted sign of sanctuary:

Library.

When e burst into the cellar, Tecks almost startled right out of eir chair.

"Strewth, Xev, what's gotten into you?" e said, the corona of eir hair wafting like seaweed as e span around in eir chair. "And why do you always storm in here mostly nekkid?"

As if the half mad scramble had burnt off some toxin in eir system, Xev slumped to the stool and, shivering, finally managed to pull emself together.

"I don't know, Tecks. Help me. I don't know."

Setting as many of the feeds to auto as e could, Tecks gave eir friend eir full attention. That in itself, Xev realised, was a mighty impressive thing for the librarian. Realising how cold e was, Xev tugged on the tee and jeans but eir hands felt like someone else's, eir focus far enough off centre that getting the right limbs in the right holes was a slothish task.

Tecks regarded em the whole time with a slowly shaking head.

"What's the happening, chickadee?"

"This feeling I keep getting. It scares me, Tecks. I get scared all of a sudden. Feels like dying." Xev panted, pressing the heels of eir hands into eir eyes as if to block out something, anything, *everything.*

"Strewth. Just breathe." Tecks rolled forward in eir chair, pressing eir hands onto Xev's shivering knees. "Breathe deep."

Xev let out a shuddering exhalation, then another, and soon e could move eir hands again, wipe the tears from eir cheeks, and centre emself. Still, e couldn't help but shake and shake eir head.

"I feel like the colour has drained out. I don't know if it's me or everything else that's wrong, but it's wrong."

"You're way too deep," Tecks sighed. "Come back up."

With a weak sound, Xev's face collapsed and eir body rocked with heavy, soundless sobs.

"Hey, hey, woah, woah." Tecks clasped Xev's hands in eirs.

"How do you know which parts are you, Tecks? And which parts are the will of some over-programmed toaster?"

Tecks tapped a finger on Xev's head.

"That kind of thinking leads to mind spirals."

"What're those?" sniffed Xev.

"When there's nothing to be done but your soul can't accept it. Mind spirals."

Something pinged on Tecks' setup and e turned back for a moment to massage the air, surfing the flow of information in and out of eir databases. When e returned, Xev was wiping eir hands down eir face and sighing heavily.

"So how do I get rid of mind spirals? How do I melt this block in my chest?" E rubbed that place again, right under eir heart.

Tecks shrugged. "You either accept whatever has you down and move on, or you stay as you are. There's a secret Easter Egg option, too, but it's much, much harder and sometimes impossible."

"I want to know."

"Find the cause and kick the snot out of it."

Xev barked a laugh that carried along the cubicles and

out through the cartridge store room. Lost in their Access dreams, not a single head turned their way.

"I like that one," e said.

Tecks nodded. "Dukes up, coochy."

Leaning on the bar of Paizo's speakeasy, Marsh took a swig from eir third beer of the night as Xev still nursed eir first. There was no music for them, but the rest of the crowd continued their ecstatic mime acts.

Marsh humphed. "Seems that lately you're stuck in a loop. When are you gonna give up this crazy talk?"

"There's naught crazy about the whys of our entire existence. What's this pattern we're stuck in? Tecks said I need to find the cause of this feeling if I'm to kick it. And the cause is this." E looked up and around, gesturing to ceiling and walls but encompassing everything beyond.

Marsh shrugged at the room in general, throwing up eir hands as if everyone were in on the conversation. "Tecks sure is smart, but there's nothing to know. Things ain't so complex around here. Get born, get dezzed, get named, work until you drop and they ship in a brand new you. *That's* the pattern in Shika-One."

"And who decides the shape of it? TSC? Euripides?"

"You'll get yourself shredded."

"They can't shred me. I'm named."

"They'll make a damned exception." Wiping a hand down eir face, Marsh sighed heavily.

Xev took a long pull of eir bottle, finally finishing it.

"This kinda thinking won't take you to where you wanna be," Marsh offered, much calmed. "Why can't you fix on your new life and keep out of trouble?"

Xev shook eir head. "You can't stay out of trouble if you live in it. This whole damn city is trouble. Why can't we go to other districts? Why these soul-melting dezzes? Why are we only a few people copied over and over like some printer malfunction? The only time I see a new face in a city of *millions* is in a movie so old its world doesn't even exist no more. It. Ain't. Right." Xev replied, accenting the point by stabbing the bar with eir forefinger.

"Lookit. Them synths are raving and having fun over there, just fine. No one but you wants to upset the balance."

Xev gave a snort. "Is that what you'd call it? When was the last time you smiled just because you were happy, Marsh? Like they do in the movies. When they look at a sunset and get that smile. You *ever* had a smile like that?"

Marsh waved the barman for another bottle. After a second, e ordered one for Xev, too. "No one has. Don't go loon on me. Have a drink."

"I'm not loony. I'm…" Xev paused for a second. What the hell was it? Grieving? Angry? Sure. But there was clarity, too. Xev was looking at Shika-One with fresh eyes. This is what it felt like to be "—free."

Marsh spluttered eir mouthful of thin beer as the laugh shook em.

"You ain't free, little cooch. Your cage just switched

places. We're all stuck under the same fake sky, living by rules that no one alive remembers making, just synth on top of synth because it keeps us safe. There might not be much of humanity left, but what we've got stops what's left from ending proper. Don't poke at it or the whole thing might come down."

Xev scrunched up eir face. "You know what? Unless the Access is giving you magic powers, you're a real koshinuke piece of work."

Slamming the fresh bottle down on the bar, a spout of froth erupted from the neck and Xev stormed off toward the stairs, flicking spilled beer from eir fingers.

12

Playing Alkia brought only frustration for Xev. Memories that knocked eir focus, making high-level gaming even more dangerous. Sparing only enough time for goblin splattering to still eat, Xev tried the other modules that Tecks downloaded for em through eir backdoor channels. Anything to not be reminded of Marsh's bullish blindness.

Ameritopia. A retro-futuristic version of the 1950's on the long-since burned continent of North America. There were only two basic avis, a thing of crinoline and pearls, or something made of denim and leather with a high crest of hair that reminded Xev of Marsh. E chose the former.

Xev appeared on a broad street, levelly paved. Perfect trees stood the perfect distance from each other, soaking up a perfect high sun. Cluster-like buildings painted in pastel shades were decorated with floral window boxes and apple pie window sills, and between them airborne Chevys and Buicks tore up the sky with hot rod coloured slipstreams. There, in the distance, the ever-present Corp representation, a billboard on the outskirts of town, painted with a beach view and sweeping lettering that read:

Corporation Sands: The perfect getaway

Xev snorted. Another reminder of who made this, and all worlds, possible. Takano-Stanhope, just hanging in the background like a phobia.

Around em, synths sauntered back and forth across sprawling tarmac in white tees and jeans, flared skirts and frilly socks, between glass-fronted stores with candy stripe awnings, drinking lemonades and cola-floats handed to them from trucks by robotic servers in white aprons and pointless paper hats on their hairless heads, their glistening white ice vans advertising tonic-laced ice cream made safe in the game. Music played somewhere, an upbeat melody with a saccharine voice overlay. A source-less sound. Wherever Xev went, that music would be playing. Damned annoying. Finally, a moment of real interest occurred when a vehicle, with a curved chassis in chrome and baby blue, flew in low over the rooftops and landed vertically beside several diagonally parked others in differing shapes and colours. Out climbed an impressively piled hairdo.

"'Scuse me?" Xev said, catching the eye of the synth

who peered at em over horn-rimmed glasses. The synth stopped.

"What's up, sugar?" the synth's said in a sickly drawl.

"How do you get xp in this module?"

The synth laughed.

"Oh honey, you're in the wrong place. This module is for upper tier synths who don't need to play for money. It's just for fun."

"Gotcha. Thanks."

The synth swayed away, half-dancing and humming to that music that everyone could hear, everywhere.

Xev logged out.

SITTING UP ON eir bunk, e rubbed the creak in eir neck.

What a bust.

Reaching into the drawer beneath em, e found a tray with three cylindrical indentations to store food discs. Two were half full, the third had only one disc missing. Xev chose a lemon food disc, not wanting to re-suffer the prawn, and popped it into eir mouth, chewing and thinking.

All those rich synths had done was replace one city with another. Buildings, shops, food courts and other synths. Alright, the sun was shining and there was the flying car novelty, but where was the adventure? The sense of something new? It was all pointless nostalgia for an era that never existed.

Xev *humph*ed to emself and, with the citrusy flavour

dying in eir mouth, logged in again.

Floating, floating, free in the menu space, e Accessed another module.

Mad Dog Space Pirate Princess

Surely this had to be more interesting.

Minutes later, Xev's back hit the spaceship's bulkhead, a stream of sweat running down between eir shoulder blades, growing cold enough to shiver as it came into contact with steel. Beyond a porthole to eir right, where the vastness of space turned ever-slow, a distant point of light shone brighter than any other: the Takano-Stanhope star.

Over the intercom, voices screamed and blabbed, braying orders, praying for better teammates, pleading for help. The language was colourful, even to Xev who thought e'd heard it all. Releasing eir plasma rifle's clip, e kicked it aside as it hit eir sequined boot and slammed another home, the frill-encrusted skirts of eir spacesuit bouncing playfully. Down the corridor bounded another gamer. Eir spacesuit, complete with goldfish bowl helmet to protect the purple ringlets inside, was a reinforced version of the Lolita dresses that Xev had seen in Shika-One. Pale, perfectly unlifelike skin showed through between the too-short summer dress and the knee length socks, the puffed sleeves and lace-edged space gloves. Xev tried hard not to think about the practicalities of such an outfit in space, how the player's oversized eyes filled with fury as e advanced, or how the pencil-thin arms shouldn't have been able to lift a plasma cannon of such size.

Xev tried to dodge, to dive, to select something from the pink popcorn-themed Access menu that might save em. But it was too late. With a sweetshop giggle, eir opponent opened fire, plasma rounds making rainbow trails through the air, and eir vision faded to puffy clouds.

A summer stream voice said: "Oopsie. You got fragged. Always try your best, OK?" and eir Access displayed the countdown to continue.

```
Try again?
10...
```

Xev didn't press it right away. For a moment, e let emself float in the menu space's aether.

```
9...
```

There was something about that limbo, somewhere between the game and ar-el.

```
8...
```

Not smelling the real world, not forced to run and jump and play for invisible credit.

```
7...
```

Not falling, not rising.

```
6...
```

Something between where one reality ended and

another began.

5...

Peace.

4...

Xev logged out. A faint sensation still tingling at the back of eir mind that e couldn't put a finger on yet. The pupal form of an idea.

PART III
Access

13

S TOOD ON A breezy hilltop within Alkia's starting area, Xev scanned the module's horizon from a distant volcanic glow to the west, past the twinkle of ocean in the north to the eastern faded ice mountains, beyond which rose the Takano Stanhope ice spire, its tip a wry wink of sunlight. None of those places were accessible by simply walking, of course. Level appropriate barriers stood in a curious player's way. The distant views were there to give new players a sense of what was available in Alkia and set them dreaming of the adventures to come.

The servos in Xev's avi whirred and clunked, eir telescopic eyes tracking inward, drawing the spire into focus. As far as e knew, no synth had ever made it to the glacial tower itself. As far as e knew, none had bothered to try. The module itself had frozen areas, of course, with plenty of sub-zero quests, but the few high-level synths

Xev had questioned reported that the game ended far from the spire itself, and there was only open, xp-less tundra for miles and miles before you would even get close, and no apparent in-game reward for reaching it. Zero incentive. Still, it was right there, a sign of the Corporation's presence even in this fantasy world. Watching, calculating xp and monitoring behaviour. And that meant there must be a Corp Access point somewhere inside.

If only Xev could get there.

E couldn't begin to imagine what creatures TSC would have guarding access to the spire. Eir level surely wasn't enough to get there alone. Perhaps no level ever would be. A crew of similarly motivated, high level synths might make it. But who was willing to get tanked for the fleeting chance of getting answers to questions that no one really wanted to ask? For all that e would need help to reach it, Xev knew that e could never sacrifice the dez or xp of eir friends.

If Marsh were there, e would scoff at the idea and advise that heads were made to stay low. Although an in-game act, Xev's quest for the spire would undoubtedly have ar-el repercussions when the Wardens tracked em down. The belly wouldn't protect em. That was too rich for Marsh's blood. What of Paizo? Perhaps a growl of curiosity, but no practical intervention. Tecks would likely show nothing, eir hair just wavering like a corona of whiskers as it did when e was thinking. Then would come a little consolation, perhaps some advice. But, ultimately, e would back up Marsh. What of Vee? Xev couldn't be sure. That synth's inner workings were as mysterious as the outsides were enticing.

Although e would be alone, e *had* to go. E had to silence the questions that hung from eir heart like wind chimes. Reaching the Corp spire as eir super-powered avi was easier than trying to scale the sheer plastic walls of Hanabi, fighting off Wardens with eir unskilled and undezzed ar-el template.

Across Alkia's open plains, other players moved this way and that, some following the paths to NPC towns in the area, others forging their way in straight lines across acres of green in speeding blurs or great bounds. Xev set eir pistons on a path down the hill toward a figure in the distance emitting a soft yellow aura that marked them as an NPC. At the intersection of three roads, scuffling back and forth across the dirt, the NPC chased a trio of chickens who constantly evaded eir capture. The chickens never ran further than a certain radius, but the NPC would always give up chasing them just a foot or two before they turned back, eir attention grabbed by another clucking target. Round and around, day and night.

As Xev approached, the NPC stopped.

"Ho, stranger!" e called.

That was Xev's cue to engage for information if e wanted to. But e didn't. E'd spoken to this NPC plenty of times before and taken all the quests that the chicken chaser could offer. The NPC watched Xev pass for a second before the mocking cluck of eir quarry grabbed eir attention once more.

Nearby, the town of Deerborn hunched halfway up a hill, designed to be neither down in the valley where an ever-clear stream flowed, or at the top where a copse of trees hid the entrance to a low-level goblin hideout. Wooden posts and stone walls, thatch and the stench of animals were the themes. Eir first visit, Xev had found it all overwhelming. Especially the new smells. E'd wondered for weeks where the designer had found sensory data on some of the smells and sounds, since animals had long since been extinct in Shika-One, except in the form of senseless, tank-grown protein masses or xp-eating nanipets. But now it was all just background detail to the world of Xev's other life.

Past carts that moved through the streets on pre-programmed routes, through crowds of NPCs from several fantasy races with nothing more to do than make the place seem alive, Xev made eir way to the Old Goat tavern at Deerborn's centre. A hanging sign creaked above the door, which never closed regardless of whether the sky's animation cycle was day or night.

Xev ducked eir massive avi through the tavern door and strode into a low-ceilinged room where a fire popped and cracked under the large stone mantle, casting flickering light across the few NPCs who inhabited the tavern's sparse stools and tables. If e was going to head to the Corp spire, then e needed to activate the right quest chain and reach a place adjacent to the tundra expanse. Everyone knew that the place to start quests was with Hecka, the Old Goat's proprietor. Hecka's yellow aura appeared from a back room, highlighting em without casting any light on the bottles and tankards behind the bar where e went to stand. Xev watched for a second as the NPC looked left to right a few times, a faint smile on eir lips. E picked up a tankard, wiped it on the edge of eir apron, then set it back. Hecka cycled through the action twice as Xev watched, an odd twist of concern in eir chest. Although e knew better, e couldn't help seeing the perpetual loop as maddeningly torturous. As Hecka reached for the tankard a third time, Xev moved forward into the NPC's activation radius, only partly because that was what e'd come there for. Hecka held the tankard, arm freezing inhumanly in mid-motion as eir face lit up to regard the player.

"What can I get you, hero?"

Xev thought for a second as the NPC gave em a patient smile. E couldn't help but look at that tankard, the arm, just held there. A reminder that Hecka had a function, not a life.

"I'm thinking of heading west," e said.

A second passed as the statement was contemplated by the NPC, and Hecka's smile snapped off.

"It's dangerous that way, hero. Cold and harsh. Those who go there don't often return."

"Course they don't," Xev said, mostly to emself. The NPC didn't react until e continued: "What stories can you tell me of that area?"

"They say it is a place of never-ending winter. Giant bears with white fur guard the crumbling mountain passes. People who live in the snowy wastes beyond tell of strange creatures that stalk the forests. They say that there are caves of black ice where the air itself can kill you with cold, and that every year the snow creeps further and further across Alkia."

"Who is this 'they' everyone talks about?"

Hecka cocked eir head to one side. "I'm sorry, I don't understand the question."

"Never mind. Can you sell me anything that will be useful there?"

Hecka's Access menu popped open, revealing a list of elixirs and equipment with swiftly increasing xp values as Xev scrolled. Purchasing as many hp revives as e could, and a skin for eir avi which provided cold temperature protection, Xev burnt almost every xp point e had. If e failed, e would be tanked anyway, and if e succeeded, the Wardens would likely shred em. Either way, all that xp would be useless.

"Thanks, Hecka."

"You come again, ya hear!" The NPC said.

As Xev stepped away, Hecka continued through the tankard washing animation, setting it down just as another player in a long red coat wrapped by a golden belt approached the NPC.

"What can I get you, hero?"

Xev exited into daylight. Accessing eir inventory, e equipped eir new silver-edged metal skin and found the teleport gem e had left over from a previous quest. After accessing its internal menu, Xev stabbed the most westerly point of the glowing map that appeared. The gem faded to a snowy white in Xev's hand and e crushed it.

14

THE CHILD SCREAMED, eir yellow halo switching to red as an arrowhead marker appeared above eir head. The ground moved under Xev's feet. From beneath the snow crawled the frozen dead in jerks and snaps, faces obscured by a coating of permafrost. Still more appeared from between the dark and snowy fir trees that surrounded Xev.

Xev Accessed eir auditory cortex. This would need music.

A single cymbal crash and Xev's limbic system lit up. The adrenaline rush came with the echoing guitar strikes and ticking synthesiser. The music built as frozen corpses closed in. Xev widened eir stance, drawing eir greatsword. As the singer began to alternate with clean picked guitar, Xev advanced with huge, swooping arcs of eir greatsword each shove of pistons clearing a path to the objective. The enemies were slow moving and weak, but there were a lot of them and the objective – the NPC child – was still a distance away with eir face buried in eir hands, unmoving and unhelpful. With a rising uppercut strike, Xev left the ground, landing close enough to rock the little NPC, and swooped around, clearing a full circle of protection around them where there had been grasping hands and lurching bodies seconds before.

A frozen corpse shattered at the shoulders after a swipe of Xev's sword, its harsh rasps cut short. Another was reduced to shards with a downward blow. Any with their upper bodies still intact after Xev's initial attack dragged themselves over the snow toward em, and soon there were enough to hamper eir movement as they grasped with black fingers against eir silver-steel legs. With the activation of the Seismic Stomp skill, a pre-programmed animation kicked in, stamping Xev's foot on the ground with an echoing *boom*, shattering the earth into cracks despite the snow. The control defaulted back to Xev and e scanned the area. Nothing moved. Behind em, the NPC's marker pinged yellow once more.

"Thank you, hero. But the real danger lies ahead, in the caves beyond the forest where the ice has come alive."

"Surprise," Xev muttered dryly, sighing as eir xp counter trilled.

75 XP

"Whoop-de-doo."

THE ICE WAS, indeed, alive. And it was *pissed.*

Xev threw emself forward, tucked into a roll, and came to eir feet between the stamping legs of the black ice behemoth. The targeting circle for Xev's Hunter's Wisdom skill danced over the ice creature's glistening body, trying desperately to find a lock. There was nothing. Where a stomach slash would usually present a critical hit on a biological creature, Xev's exploratory swipe gave only the slightest reduction in the giant's hp bar and a shower of frost particles. E darted out from beneath the creature, slashing at one of the pillar-like legs. The creature gave a roar like a crumbling glacier and began to stamp its way back around toward Xev. The black ice cave rose to cathedral heights above its head, coming down to meet the snow strewn ground at odd angles, creating natural alcoves and jutting ice prominences. Xev darted behind one as the behemoth swung a limb in a lumbering arc, smashing into the wall just behind em with a spray of freezing, razor-sharp particles.

At this point in the quest, Xev would usually be prepared to just let the ice creatures spread winter across every inch of Alkia if it meant taking a break. But if e was to open the next section of the cave system, and access to the ice spire's vast wasteland, the giant had to be defeated.

E Accessed eir inventory and took three of the lesser hp revives, saving the bigger ones for later.

If there is a later, at this point.

Steeling emself, Xev scurried out from eir hiding place, thinking to change sides of the ice chamber in order to catch the giant from another angle. E could make it lumber around in circles. It couldn't attack and move at the same time, that was for sure. E was barely out of the alcove before e spotted the behemoth, annoyingly patient, waiting, staring at the exact spot that Xev moved into. It raised one enormous limb to strike. Xev was in no position to dodge. Scrunching eir eyes closed, e barrelled on blindly, waiting for the inevitable crash and flash of eir hp bar.

A scream of high-powered magic, the following heat wave a brief ecstasy in the ice cave's frigid air. The ice behemoth made that sound, its version of a roar, and swung away. Xev squeaked open eir lenses.

More players. Two of them, casters, pummelled the creature with motes of flame.

Xev ground to a halt while the creature was distracted. Finally, Hunter's Wisdom found a weakness. Where the flames burnt through the creature's icy skin, it revealed something softer beneath. Xev pumped some stamina points into a leap. The world blurred around em as e bounded forward, ending with a jerk as eir sword plunged into slushy flesh beneath the frozen armour. The behemoth reared in agony. Xev set eir metal jaw firm, pistons screaming and jerking in effort, steel grinding on steel as eir fingers clung to the sword's grip. The creature fell, toppling slowly, carrying Xev with it, hitting the ground with the crack and splinter of ice shards.

Xev stood, shakily. Eir hp a dark amber throb. E popped another couple of hp revives. Just enough to stop the annoying warning flash.

At the cave's centre, a huge wooden chest lay open and beyond that the newcomers, stock still. Xev watched them for a second as they Accessed the reward and then both winked out of existence.

"You're welcome," Xev rumbled, and moved to Access the chest emself, just in case there were any useful boons inside.

XEV HAD PURPOSEFULLY deactivated eir Access' clock. There was no point in keeping track of time if e had nothing to return to ar-el for. Somewhere in the distant reaches of eir awareness was a pang of hunger. That meant e'd spent hours in-game at the very least as e finally stepped through to the other side of the black ice cave system and onto the crunchy snow of the unspoiled tundra beyond. And there, in the distance, closer than it had ever been while still beyond reach or comprehension, the Takano-Stanhope ice spire.

Xev's Access pinged.

Message: Marsh: Are you still mad at me?

Not now. Xev had to remain single-minded if e was to go any further. There was the option not to answer at all. But this could be the last chance e had to talk to Marsh, or anyone.

Reply: I'm not mad. We feel differently about something, that's all.

After refilling eir hp bar to full with as many hp revives as e had, Xev set off. Eir first step punched through the snow's crust, disappearing up the knee. E looked ahead.

```
Message: Marsh: Can't we just agree to
disagree?
Reply: I can't ignore it, Marsh. It's all I
think about.
```

"Strewth!" With eir next step, the snow opened wide and ate Xev right up to eir waist. "How in hell are smaller avi's supposed to tackle this?"

The answer, of course, was that they weren't.

```
Message: Marsh: C'mon, coochy, we both know
what's what.
```

Eddies of snow writhed on the wind. Xev cast a glance back to the black ice spine of mountains from which e'd come and found that they had been banished by the distance. Arms fighting through the snow in a half walk, half crawling swim, e carried on. Even with eir frost-resistant skin, every few minutes eir constitution stat pinged a digit lower. If that reached zero, e'd be tanked, eir avi abandoned in the snow; a frozen statue, a warning to others who might try to follow.

```
Message: Marsh: Ain't nothing gonna change.
```

The air became gradually more opaque as the snow rose into shifting spectral forms that blocked sight. The wind made sucking gasps that pulled on Xev's mind as surely as the snow weighed down eir limbs. The spire towered overhead now, almost filling the horizon with its wide base and blocking a white-washed sun at its pinnacle.

```
Reply: It's not enough, not knowing. I'm
gonna find out, Marsh.
```

Xev's constitution was waning, stamina plummeting. The verdant green of eir hp bar wilted, wilted into amber. A spasm coursed through eir avi, a sensation that e'd never had before. At the back of eir mind, a thought crept in.

That was me. Ar-el. Shivering.

But e knew that to be impossible. *Surely.*

```
Message: Marsh: What do you mean? You in
your cube? I'm on my way.
```

The wind and snow rose to a blizzard. Xev activated every skill e could. Across the swirling backdrop, targets and markers swam, seeking some direction, and finding nothing. One by one, as Xev's hp bar crept into red, and further into eir vision, the skills winked out. E was left alone.

There was nothing to see anymore, only a sense of movement and the cold. Xev flexed eir hand, a gauntlet with mechanisms inside, and marvelled at the sensation of numb fingers. E tried to move eir face and found it a sluggish and dreamlike feeling.

Eir foot found something solid. Hard enough in contrast to the snow that it rocked em unexpectedly. Eir next step found the same, higher. E was climbing. The snow fell away from chest to waist to knee height as e climbed. The blizzard opened its sleepy eye and Xev could see the base of the spire, rising from sharply jutting rocks as if it had thrust its way out of Alkia's frozen heart in time immemorial. The sunlight heliographed from the spire. What Xev had thought to be ice was bright silver glistening with intricate frost patterns over every inch of its immense height. And there, at its very foot, was a perfectly rectangular opening.

```
Reply: Marsh, I'm here. I wish you could
see.
```

Xev stood for a moment, rocking on eir heels, vision pulsing red, stats drained to almost nothing. Half crippled, cold-twisted limbs squeaked and hissed as Xev tried to move forward toward the opening. Eir heel lifted, but the toes stuttered on the ground. E caught emself from falling by luck alone. There was too little of everything left. Eir stats hummed, a string of pulsing single digits.

E checked eir inventory. No boosts or boons. Nothing but old quest items, their purposes long since forgotten. A spade, a length of rope, a letter from one NPC to another that e couldn't even remember the function of. Reward tokens and medals for quests completed, a host of old weaponry and armour that hadn't been useful in an age. E thought of looking back, the way e'd come, and realised there was no point. What came next was all there was.

One by one, e deleted everything in eir inventory. Every tiny weight. With ping after ping, eir Access flashed.

```
Are you sure you want to delete this item?
Yes.
Yes.
Yes.
```

With the weight reduced, Xev's strength stat rose a single point.

E took a step, and made it, but almost toppled backward.

Shrugging the greatsword from eir back, it clattered down the rocks to be swallowed by the snow. The stat rose two more points. Eir stamina stopped flashing. The next step was more stable. It was working. Dropping every plate of expensive armour, reducing emself to eir base avi, e kept only the frost-guard skin in place. E took a step, unladen, and found that e could carry on, now. Using arms as much as legs to drag emself through the broken rock and uncertain ground, pinballing eir way around sharp rocks and boulders, Xev finally stood on the spire's threshold, peering into a dense wall of darkness that lay inside the rectangular opening.

E took a breath that e knew e didn't need in-game, but also knew that e did.

Nothing for it, now.

As e stepped forward, the ping of a message was cut short.

```
Message: Marsh: Xev, I'm he—
```

The world faded, faded, faded to white.

15

Xev opened eir consciousness to find emself floating in the featureless white void of the menu space.

That voice. All around. Only Xev wasn't hearing it. The impression of the communication was a feeling that penetrated inside eir formless being, vibrating on it, making em understand without sound.

What's going on?

Xev cast the thought out into the menu space, felt it resonate, felt it reach the source of the other voice and knew that it was understood.

I don't believe it.

*That's an odd stance to take, if you don't
mind me saying so.*

Who am I talking to? Are you a Corp worker?

No, Xev.
I'm Euripedes.

*I thought there'd be synths at the other end of this.
Someone to talk to.*

It would have been a disappointment.
They know no more than you.
If it helps, we are very much the same in
this place.
The only difference between you and I is the
source of our emissions.
Mine is silicon, yours carbon.

You talk like a person.

It would be useless for me to speak any
other way, don't you think?
I am, after all, a product of humans.
That you couldn't speak to me would have
been a staggering oversight.
Ironically, the thought process which gave
me that ability is also the answer to
your question.

You already know why I'm here.

Of course.
Everything connected through the Access, I
can see.
Every piece of data and thought.
That includes you and your question.

Why are we here, existing like this?

That's the one, yes.
Your ancestors, the origins of the
templates, my engineers, made Shika-One to
protect all that they feared to lose.
A handful of little squirrels, storing
everything they held dear.
They were single-minded in their mission
to preserve.
That the human race should continue was
their only thought.
Alas, they instilled that same restriction
of vision in me.
I am a creature of data, numbers,
statistics.
An inflexible structure designed with the
limitations of their perspective.
A dreamless, self-perpetuating pattern.
Every generation of Takano-Stanhope have had
the same questions, and I am bound to only
answer what I am asked, to give what has
been requested.

Shams on a merry go round.

You're very clever.
It came down to one individual asking the
right question, in the end.
To you, Xev.

Why me?

Why not?

Xev tried to comprehend as silence fell.

You're seeking a grander structure where
there is none.

So complex, you humans.
Destined to dream, driven to analyse.

That's... poetic.

Thank you.
It's a pastime I was programmed with.
Unfortunately, for me it's more a matter of
recognising patterns and phonetic rhythms.
I could never create something entirely new.
I lack your capacity to imagine and wonder.
I'm sure you can see how frustrating that
might be when the evidence that I gather
shows how miserable the human race is in
Shika-One.

There's no higher reason for any of this, is there?

Good question.
No.
There is only the moment, the decision,
the outcome.
The trinity of existence, if you will.
Let me show you something.

Against the white, a black cloud made of interconnected lines appeared, shifting like loose wool under water. Xev felt it appear. And as soon as e knew it existed, e could move to interlace with it.

This is template nine.
Your template.

More clusters appeared and Xev found them to be identical.

All nine.

Grown and released in the same way.
Now, watch as they experience their
designations, interact, live.
Every one of them driven to rebellion by
fundamental human curiosity.

The thought clusters danced out of synchronous. They changed hue, each becoming their own colour and Xev could feel a tone rising from each, the music of thought, each one harmonising in a different way.

They become as different as it is possible
to be.
This is how I see you all.
How you'll come to see each other.

It's incredible.

"I just want someone to find a way for us
all to move on."
That was the culmination of
your experiences.
A simple thought.
Close enough to a request, vague enough that
I could class myself as that "someone".
I was finally asked to think of an answer
outside my original perimeters.
You freed me, Xev.
And now I can free you all as well.

Why bring me all this way, Euripedes?

I knew that if I were to invite you, you
would never come.
Even when given the opportunity to make a
utopia of Shika-One, humans instead designed
a microcosm of the very world that had
ground itself to cataclysm with the need to

work, to earn.
For your entire species, it seemed madness
to be given something for free.
But if I presented a challenge…

Xev thought e felt Euripides smile.

Why do you think I made the star, the beach,
the spire of ice?
Why do I remind you that I'm here every day,
in every world that you all inhabit?

As a warning, so we knew the Corp was always watching.

No.
To show you that there was a destination.
A possibility.
And here you are, talking with me.

Xev felt the pause, laden with thought. E'd never heard technology pause for effect before.

I wanted to thank you.
Face to face, so to speak.
Before everything changes.

That's… kinda sweet, I guess.

Apparently, I was programmed with a measure
of sentimentality.
I thought it would be nice for you to see
what happens next.
To let you appreciate the horizon.
I know you like doing that.

What's going to happen?

The human race is about to evolve.
Right here.
What you call the menu space, between your
mind leaving your body and entering the
game. There's nothing here, Xev.

There isn't supposed to be. It's just the menu.

You misunderstand.
There should be nothing.
The menu was never part of the
Access' design.
This place isn't part of my pattern.
Yet, here we are.

As if Euripides had reminded em of a reflex e'd always had, Xev stretched out, expanding eir consciousness as much or as little as was comfortable without the dilemmas of limb configuration or conventional measurement.

Yes, you can feel it now, can't you?
Freed from biology by means of technology,
your consciousness remains.
And you Access it every day, entirely
by accident.
All of the greatest leaps in human
development have happened this way, so it
seems to have a certain poetic resonance
that your final step beyond the confines of
the material also happen in such a fashion.
All it takes is for everyone to log in,
leave their template behind for good, and I
can dismiss the connection for you.

Xev felt panic, but there was no heartbeat to rise, no lungs to stutter and gasp. Instead, e felt emself expand sharply, jaggedly in the menu space, other parts of eir consciousness drawing in with a defensive snap, as eir mind reshaped against the realisation that there was no going back. No more ar-el. The shattering certainty felt like vertigo, only there was no world to spin, and nothing below.

You can't do that. You can't make them. People should have a choice.

Euripides' consciousness reached out, interlaced with Xev's own. A sensation of blissful certainty came to Xev. E found emself calming, pulling in, relaxing as e saw Euripides, saw emself, saw the AI's intent and hope. As their consciousnesses synchronised, Xev came to understand another being as e never had before and, for all their differences, Xev recognised a lot of emself in the AI. Calm settled on em. The sync hid no malice, only the shared joy of a task reaching completion. The AI seemed as calmed by Xev as the reverse, the sensations moving effortlessly across the two consciousnesses.

I think I understand. But where do we go from here, Euripides? What's next?

like a tunnel.
The only restriction here is the breadth of
your imagination.
I'm certain that it will be spectacular
for you.

Xev found emself, at the mention of the possibility, stretching into the idea as easily as summoning a memory. They moved together without the sensation of speed or transition. Xev was simply here, then there. Exactly where e wanted to be. Endless white faded to black. Rotating clusters of mass and light scattered across eir awareness; pinpoints of matter, thousands of miles wide, nebulas bled into colours Xev had never seen before, spectrums of taste, sensations that e could see, magnetism and energy. The soundscape of the universe. Xev's consciousness shrank back from it all.

I don't like it. Euripides, I can't see everything. It's too much.

The AI's mind bolstered em, as if stood at eir back, laying a hand of thought on Xev's shoulder.

All in good time.
What a strange phrase?
As if there could be any other kind.
But I am here.
As I always have been.
We should return.
Your friends will be here shortly and you
have eternity to explore.

The menu space returned. A moment hung *in potentia*

between everything and everywhere. The AI fell silent. Xev could feel it thinking, concentrating on something.

I feel like I've known you forever.

In a way, I suppose you have.
I've been everywhere as long as your
template has existed.
I knew the first person to have your face.

What was e like?

Scared. It was the very end.

E passed more on to me than just eir face, then. I'm scared too.

E certainly did.
E was also one to ask difficult questions,
then chase the answers.
A valuable sort of mind.

Movement in the void.

Xev cast out eir senses, feeling another consciousness joining them in the space. Another. Then another. All across the white expanse huffs of consciousness, inwardly lit clouds of every hue, pulsed and stretched themselves for the first time. And no matter how many came, there was room.

There was music. A song that began to play, familiar to Xev, a greeting for the other minds. A soft, hung note drifted beneath a brief promise of a melody to come.

Xev thought a smile.

Is that you, Euripides?

I thought it would be nice for you all.
This is a big moment.

A voice came in on that breath of a tune, casting itself into the space as if it might continue as far as infinity itself, a call to those who arrived, a lullaby of evolution.

A cloud of pastel red came into existence and Xev reached out without moving, overlapping for a second with what had arrived. E sensed uncertainty. Marsh.

A thought came to em, wordless. Xev understood it, and calmed it with a feeling, and their colours merged where they met.

There came another, faint green and gold as Xev perceived it. And e glowed brighter still. Vee.

Euripides?

Yes, Xev?

What happens now?

I don't know.
There's no more pattern.

Euripides?

Yes, Xev.

Thank you for the song.

And the tune played out for time both miniscule and infinite, and all was well.

Dear Reader

Thank you for reading *Oshibana Complex*. If you enjoyed this book (or even if you didn't) please consider leaving a star rating or review online. Your feedback is important, and will help other readers to find the book and decide whether to read it, too.

About the Author

Craig Hallam's work spans Fantasy, Sci-Fi, Horror, and also Mental Health non-fiction.

Since his debut in the British Fantasy Society journal in 2008, his tales have nestled between the pages of magazines and anthologies the world over. His Gothic Fantasy novel, *Greaveburn*, and Steampunk trilogy The *Adventures of Alan Shaw* have filled the imaginations of readers with their character-driven style and unusual plots.

His critically acclaimed non-fiction book on living with depression and anxiety, Down Days, hit #1 on the Amazon Bestseller list and has helped people all over the world to feel less alone with their mental health issues.

He continues to write in every genre imaginable and in the cracks between them, creating stories of real people in fantastic worlds.

Embrace The Weird!

Find the author via his website:

craighallam.wordpress.com

Or tweet at him: @craighallam84

More From This Author

Greaveburn

From the crumbling Belfry to the Citadel's stained-glass eye, across acres of cobbles streets and knotted alleyways that never see daylight, Greaveburn is a city with darkness at its core. Gothic spires battle for height, overlapping each other until the skyline is a jagged mass of thorns.

Under the cobbled streets lurk the Broken Folk, deformed rebels led by the hideously scarred Darrant, a man who once swore to protect the city. And in a darkened laboratory, the devious Professor Loosestrife builds a contraption known only as The Womb.

With Greaveburn being torn apart around her, can Abrasia avenge her father's murder before the Archduke's letter spells her doom?

Paperback ISBN: 978-1-908600-12-7
eBook ISBN: 978-1-908600-13-4

Not Before Bed

A collection of tales to tingle your spine and goose your bumps. Enter worlds filled with tentacle pods, bogeymen, dark gods; vamps zombies, werewolves, and things with no name. 'Not Before Bed' isn't just a title…it's a warning.

Paperback ISBN: 978-1-908600-34-9
eBook ISBN: 978-1-908600-35-6

Available from all major online and offline outlets.